The Garden House

Linda Mahkovec

Other books by Linda Mahkovec

The Dreams of Youth

Seven Tales of Love

The Christmastime Series

Christmastime 1940: A Love Story

Christmastime 1941: A Love Story

Christmastime 1942: A Love Story

Christmastime 1943: A Love Story

The Garden House
by Linda Mahkovec

...

Copyright © 2015

ISBN-10:1-946229-12-1
ISBN-13: 978-1-946229-12-0

Distributed by Bublish, Inc.

Cover Design by Laura Duy
© Colin Young/Dreamstime

To my family.
And to all lovers and creators of
beauty, gardens, and home.

Chapter 1

~

Miranda awoke to the darkness of early morning. A barely-there breeze softly swelled the curtains, causing the sheers to billow as if in slow motion. Before going to bed, she had opened the window and parted the curtains, to better hear the sounds of the night and the morning birdsong. But at this hour all was hushed, except for the rhythmic breathing of her husband. The troubling sense of yearning, that of late had kept her company, had awakened with her. She slipped off the comforter, and walked to the window.

She lightly rubbed her bare arms. In the garden below, only the white flowers were visible – cone-shaped hydrangeas, discs of Queen Anne's lace, full-blossomed peonies – dream flowers of night. They appeared weightless, as if they hovered in timeless-ness, and would not attach to the stems and roots until the fuller light of morning connected them. Further down, the garden house loomed out of the darkness – like the flowers, not yet anchored, still in silent communion with the night. As she rested her eyes on it, almost imperceptibly it shifted – from pale gray to the beginnings of white, gaining in shape and substance as dawn gave way to day. Now she could make out the blue trim, the window boxes. Soon it would stand firm in the bright light of morning.

Everything was right there – in the tenuous linking of night with dawn, in the garden house full of memories, in the flowers and paths of the garden, in the longing that spilled out into it all. It was as if she were looking at a puzzle, and almost had it pieced together while it lingered at the edge of night – but then it completely disappeared with the morning light, as if it had never existed.

Breakfast. She would make breakfast.

She dressed quietly, washed up, and went downstairs. As she got out the eggs, milk, and butter, she tried to brush away the webby sense of discontent that clung about her. A nudging that she should be doing something more now. That her old role had changed and she must also change, or risk slipping into vagueness.

Into a large blue bowl she cracked the eggs, and added milk, vanilla, a touch of sugar. Then she began dipping slices of bread into the mix and placing them in a pan sizzling with butter.

While they browned, she turned on the tea kettle. She reached for the coffee press, and opened the bag of coffee – lifting it to her nose and taking in the rich aroma before measuring it out. The scent alone warmed her to morning, made her eager to begin the day. She took out several oranges and began slicing them to squeeze for juice. While she prepared breakfast, she heard the shower running. She smiled. The scent must have drifted upstairs.

Cooking grounded her, rooted her, in the same way gardening did. And Ben. And the kids. She caught the spray of citrus mixing with the aroma of fresh coffee, and moved more briskly as she began to set the table.

She filled a few ramekins with jams and sour cream, and poured maple syrup into a small beaker. Then she took out a bowl and filled it with strawberries and blueberries. She looked at the table and wanted it to be fuller, richer. She lifted the bright pink kalanchoe from the window shelves, and set it on the table. Too bad the kids weren't there to enjoy it. Clara would love the way the flowering plant matched the quilted placemats. And Michael would appreciate the mound of French toast dusted with powdered sugar; he had his father's love of big breakfasts.

With one hand on the counter, she gazed at the table, secure now in the routines of her kitchen, of good food, of color and light, a prettily laid table. She leaned her head to one side and studied the setting as if it were a painting, and briefly imagined herself sitting at the table, wearing a long kimono-like robe – peacock blue, or perhaps a pattern in pinks and orange.

She glanced down at her sweat pants and t-shirt. Well, they were more practical for cooking, she told herself. Still, she wished she blended more with the arrangement – the one of the table, as well as the one in her head.

Miranda smiled at Ben's quickness of step coming downstairs. She could always count on his appetite.

"Smells wonderful!" Ben said, entering the kitchen and giving her a quick kiss. He stared at the table. "All this for us? On a weekday?"

Miranda lifted and dropped one shoulder. "I was up early so I thought I'd make breakfast."

"I'm not complaining." Ben took his seat at the table and poured the steaming coffee into their cups.

Miranda sat down and looked at the ceiling-to-floor shelves behind Ben, a sort of small greenhouse that jutted out into the garden. It always filled her with happiness – the photos of the kids among the flowering plants, painted boxes and vases and tiny candles scattered throughout. But this morning, as a backdrop to the breakfast table, it filled her with melancholy.

She took a slice of French toast and poured some maple syrup over it and added a few strawberries. "I don't think I'll ever get used to cooking for just two."

"It'll just take some time," said Ben, as he drizzled syrup over his French toast.

"I suppose so."

Ben looked over at Miranda, her tone at odds with the enthusiastic breakfast spread.

"I think I'll get started on the cupboards and closets," she said. "Paula has been asking me to hand over any of my old pieces that are gathering dust. I told her with the kids gone, I was going to clean house and get rid of things. She seems to think my old paintings and sculptures will sell at her stores. You know how she can make anything look good. I doubt if they'll sell, but I guess it's worth a try."

"I'm sure she's right. Your work is great. I always tell you that, but you never believe me."

"That's because you're partial, Ben."

"Can't fault me for good taste."

"Hmm," Miranda responded with skepticism. "I guess I'll show her my old stuff, but what I really want to do is set up the studio and get started on some new things."

"Oh, that reminds me," said Ben. "I think I found a renter for the garden house for the summer."

Miranda put her fork down. "I thought we decided against it."

Ben looked up. "We did? I thought the plan was to rent it out until we were ready to put up that wall, make some of those changes we talked about."

"Ben, that was months ago. I told you just last week that I wanted to use it as a studio this summer. I want to finish that screen, for one thing. And I haven't done any painting in years."

"Miranda, I cut the boards for that screen two years ago." Ben's hand hesitated over the berries. Berries or jam? He decided on a few mixed berries and sprinkled them over another piece of French toast.

"I know. And now that I have some time, I can finally finish it."

"So I'll tell the guy it's not available." He lifted the coffee press and refilled his cup. "Oh, remember to set out Michael's camping gear if you come across it. He wants us to take it to him the next time we're down. Apparently, his new girlfriend – Casey? – is a hiker and camper." He raised his eyebrows at Miranda and grinned. "He sounds pretty happy. Portland was definitely the right choice for him."

"Caitlin," said Miranda. She placed an elbow on the table and rested her chin in her hand, lightly tapping her lips with her knuckles. She took a deep breath and resumed eating. "No. Don't tell him."

Ben raised his head. "Tell who what?"

"The tenant. The guy."

"Oh. You sure? I thought you just said – "

"No. That can wait. The rent will help with the renovations." She took another slice of French toast and spread on some sour cream and raspberry jam. "So who is he?"

"Somebody Doug knows. Or his wife, rather. A teacher or journalist or something." He looked up, trying to remember if there was anything else he knew about him. "From out East. New York, I think," he said, as if that summed it all up.

Miranda made a small sound of exasperation. "Is that all you know about him? How old is he? Is he married? Kids? What's he like? What does he teach?"

Ben drew a blank at each question.

"What's his name?"

"William. Something. Been teaching for thirty years. I don't think he's arriving until next week. I'll find out more today and let you know." He tried to read the expression on Miranda's face – far-off look, slight frown. He had been sure that his news of a tenant would make her happy. "What?"

"Nothing. It's just that – I thought that *if* we rented it out, it would be nice to have a woman. An artist. Maybe someone with a small child or two. Wouldn't that be nice? To have kids down there? Just on a temporary basis."

"You can always turn it into a daycare center if that's what you want." His suggestion, as he knew it would be, was met with a sharp glance from Miranda. "I mean it," he continued. "The kids are gone, and now you finally have some time to do what you want to do. If it's a daycare you want – "

"I don't want to run a daycare."

"Well, you did a few years ago. Don't you remember? You had plans to – "

"Well, I don't now. That's the whole point, Ben. I want to start doing some of the things I've been putting off for the last twenty-five years." As soon as the words were out, she regretted them. Ben would think she was blaming him for why she hadn't pursued her dreams, even though it had been her idea to leave school when they got married and work while Ben finished his degree.

Ben looked down at his plate, and then up at Miranda. "I know. I'm behind you on that. Just – tell me what it is you want to do, and I'll help you with it."

Miranda's eyes filled with worry. "That's just it, Ben. I don't know. I really don't. How can I have gotten to this age and not know what I want to do?" She glanced about as she searched for an answer. "What if all those things they say about middle age are true? What if I get foggy-brained and too tired to accomplish anything ever again? And I just keep gaining weight and – "

Ben laughed and leaned over to rub her shoulder. "Aw, c'mon. What are you so worried about? You just keep getting better and better. I never could keep up with you."

"Ha! You haven't gained a pound. While I – " she shook her head at the unfinished thought. "Though I do think the dry cleaner is partly to blame – everything comes back smaller. More coffee?" she asked, preventing any chance of a rebuttal.

Ben smiled and held up his cup. "Take your time and think about the tenant. You can always say no. It's completely your call."

She watched him fix another piece of French toast. "No. It's a good idea. I'm not quite ready to paint or whatever, anyway. It's going to take me weeks, maybe months, to really clean out closets and organize everything. A tenant makes sense. I'll work on the garden house today, get it ready for him. It needs a few things." She heard herself and almost cringed, as if another delay in her plans was exactly what she wanted.

Ben caught the wistful tone behind her words. "Hey – how about dinner tonight?" he asked. "At McMillans – watch the sun set on the lake. You'll have your hands full today; this way you won't have to think about cooking."

"You know me well," she said, stretching her legs and resting them on his lap. Miranda loved the restaurant's seasonal menu and always looked forward to a new culinary experience – a fresh way of preparing a vegetable, an unusual combination of herbs or spices, or a completely new dish that she would later try to recreate.

Ben's phone rang and he glanced at the number. "Sam."

He chatted with his old friend, rubbing Miranda's legs as he talked, stopping and starting in pace with the conversation.

Miranda picked a few berries from the bowl, eating them one at a time, and watched Ben, always so animated and energetic. After all these years, she thought, I'm still wild about him. He doesn't even have to do anything. He can just sit there and eat and talk on the phone and laugh – and it all makes me love him so much. He was agreeing to something, raising his eyebrows at her at some good news. She just hoped it didn't involve fishing.

Ben speared one last slice and shrugged at Miranda, as if it was so delicious he couldn't help himself. He poured out some syrup, gave a chuckle, and nodded again. "Sounds good. I'll tell her – she'll love it. See ya, buddy." He slipped the phone into his pocket.

"What will I love?"

"He invited us to his new place on the peninsula. Another month or so and it'll be ready. Doesn't that sound great?" He cast an imaginary fishing line.

A weak smile formed on her lips.

"Hiking, fishing, sitting around the fire pit at night. He said he's discovered a local berry farm that you'll love."

Miranda smiled at the cozy vision. "That does sound nice." Dear ole Sam, she thought. Always sure to include something she would enjoy.

Ben took one last bite and scooted his chair from the table. Then he took his jacket from the hall tree and headed out the door.

Miranda followed him outside, rubbing her arms against the chill. "I'll make a reservation. What time should I say?"

"Better make it 8:00. See you there." He squeezed her goodbye, intensifying his embrace until he got the laugh he was looking for.

She walked out on the flagstones and watched him drive off. A trip to the peninsula might be a good idea, after all. It would be beautiful there. She loved the deep forest walks, the smell of wood fire at night. And Sam was always good company. Though only ten years older than Ben, Sam was in many ways his mentor. She would always be grateful to him for helping Ben through a tough time. The memory of those years, of the stress Ben was under, still filled her with pain. At one point she feared he was heading for a breakdown. Long hours, corporate politics, an ever-increasing work load. It was Sam who convinced him to leave the firm and work with a smaller architect company. And it had changed their lives.

A weekend with Sam would be good for them. She could walk along the shore while they fished. After all, she'd been wanting to exercise more, get back into shape. Here was her chance. Why did she always meet everything with such resistance? Like the idea of a tenant. That, too, might be a good thing. I used to be more open, more adventurous, she thought. When did that change?

Miranda lifted her face to the sun. She loved the way the garden smelled in the early morning, the earthy dampness from the light Seattle rain, the whiff of pine, the sun just beginning to release a hint of jasmine from the trellis. And if she leaned in close enough to the roses – she cupped her hands around the dewy pinkness, buried her face in the flower, and closed her eyes at such sweetness. She often wished they could move their bed out here, sleep under the stars, put up a little canopy against the rain –

"Hey, neighbor!"

There was Paula, waving to her.

"Good morning!" called Miranda, and crossed over to where Paula was planting flowers along her wooden fence.

Paula stood and held up a potted flower. "Just look at this clematis – it's as big as a saucer."

Miranda reached out to touch the pale purple flower. "It's beautiful."

"Just got it at the nursery yesterday. They still have some left."

"I'll go this morning. I need to get flowers for the window boxes," she said, gesturing to the garden house. "I think we've found a renter for the summer."

Paula inclined her head. "I thought you were going to use it as a studio."

"We changed our minds. I want to organize the house first. Then think about what I want to do with the garden house."

"I hope that doesn't mean you're going to postpone your plans again. I remember a time when you were always working on some painting or sculpture or something."

"Yeah, well – that was ages ago."

"What is it you're afraid of? What's stopping you?"

Miranda laughed at the ridiculous notion. "I'm not afraid of anything, Paula. It's just – I haven't done anything for so long, and…"

Paula put a hand on her hip. "Does this have anything to do with turning fifty?"

"No, of course not. No. Not at all. It's just – I'm not sure if I can tap into that part of myself again. I think it might be gone."

"I don't believe that for a moment. It's in there. You just need to dig." And with that, she knelt back down and shoved the trowel into the ground. "So who's the tenant? A young painter with a five-year old child?"

Miranda laughed at the details of her earlier vision. "No, an older man. A teacher."

"Well, you can still move ahead with your plans. No reason you can't paint outside or in the garage."

"First I want to organize the house. Now that the kids are gone, I can clear out old stuff, get rid of things. And then think about painting or whatever."

Paula gave a skeptical raise of her eyebrows.

Miranda pushed her foot at a clump of grass along the fence. "I think it will help me to focus, to start with a clean slate. I have so much stuff – old pieces I've held onto, half-finished projects. I want to lighten my load, and start fresh, you know? Then maybe by the fall or so I can be ready to really work."

"Hmm. Well, don't throw away anything without letting me check it out first. The new shop opens in a month. I need to fill it up, and your things would add just the right touch."

"I doubt if there's anything you can use, but I'll start going through things."

"You really should start on something new, as well. You'll have the time now."

"Yeah." Miranda nodded and looked around. "Well, I better get started with everything. See you later." She began to walk back to the house.

"Don't wait too long, Miranda!"

Miranda turned and waited for a final word of reprimand.

But Paula was holding up the pale purple clematis. "They're sure to go fast."

Chapter 2

~

At the nursery, Miranda's cart burst with color and variety: several trays of mixed red, orange, and magenta impatiens; pots of red, pink, and white geraniums; deep blue periwinkle and yellow begonias, and two of the purple clematis for around the garden house door. She came across a variety of petunia she hadn't seen before, and added it to the cart. She always had a hard time stopping, once at the nursery. Every plant seemed to call to her – like the purple alyssum that would match so nicely. She broke apart a few trays and arranged them around the clematis, and took a step back to imagine how they would look in the planter – then she added some white alyssum for contrast. And might as well get some marigolds, she thought; they'll bloom well into the fall.

As she loaded the cartons of flowers into her car, she realized that, just like the French toast, she had overdone it. It would take her all day to plant so many flowers.

By late afternoon, she had planted the window boxes, several pots of flowers, and on either side of the door, two tubs of alyssum and clematis. After watering them all, she hauled down a bench from the garden and set it next to the door. She stood back and admired her work. It was beautiful. She wondered if the older teacher would appreciate it. No matter. It gave her pleasure to see it looking so pretty, and it brought her one step closer to having it fixed up as a studio.

She went inside the garden house and began to clean, sweeping and dusting. Though she tried to ignore the pile of wood and canvas for the screen, it stared at her from the corner, asking for completion. It would have to wait. She rolled up the canvas, and used the wood slats to prop open the door. The day had grown warm and she welcomed the light breeze.

Tired now, she sat down on the floor, resting her elbows on her knees. Then with a sigh of fatigue she stretched out, the hardwood floor feeling good against her sore back. She gazed up at the shifting shadows of leaves and branches on the ceiling and wall. I could trace them, she thought – paint them in gold and pale green. It could be beautiful.

She let her eyes wander over the details of her beloved garden house – the deep, forget-me-not blue of the dresser and window trim, the pillows and curtains she and Clara had made. They had spent so many hours over the years down here – painting, sewing, little by little transforming the run-down structure into a charming, livable cottage.

Clara had loved the profusion of forget-me-nots that surrounded the garden house, and decided to christen the cottage the Forget-Me-Not House. It had seen many tea parties and birthday celebrations, and Clara's favorite, the fairy parties. Ben and Michael were always good sports about helping out – lighting lanterns throughout the garden, tying fluttering ribbons from the trees.

Michael had also used the garden house for his share of sleepovers and parties. Miranda smiled as she remembered the pirate-themed treasure hunt for his eighth birthday. She and Ben had painted black whiskers and heavy eyebrows on the little boys, wound bandanas around their heads, and sent them off with the first clue. The tiny band of boys made their way through cottony spiders' dens, and over the River of Forgetfulness. The final clue led to a Halloween skeleton, whose bony finger pointed to the half-buried treasure chest. She would never forget the cries of joy as the boys brushed off the dried leaves, opened the lid, and beheld the

gold chocolate coins, toys, and shiny plastic dou-
bloons. And her utter surprise at their delight in
the play jewelry she had draped inside the trunk.
The boys had proudly claimed the booty, looping
strands of plastic pearls and bright purple and
green Mardi Gras beads around their necks, the
jewelry adding a strange feminine touch to their
little-boy wildness.

A sense of loss welled up inside her. Those
times were long gone. Michael and Clara were
gone. Grown. Making their way in the world. She
was happy for them, happy that they were entering
a new phase in their lives. She pressed on her eyes
to push down the tears.

A car pulled into the driveway up at the house,
and a young man checked a piece of paper against
the address. He then parked, and walked up to the
house. He was dressed in jeans and a button-down
shirt with the sleeves rolled up against the warmth –
and yet there was an air of formality about him.

He knocked at the door in a tentative manner,
took a step back, and waited. After a few moments,
he rang the doorbell, and again stepped back from
the door, with his hands linked behind him.

Turning to the side, as if indecisive about
what to do, he noticed the flagstones that led to
the side of the house. He followed them, and down
below saw a small cottage with the door propped
open. He hesitated a moment, glanced back at the

house, and then made his way down the steps to the garden house.

He walked onto the cottage's low wooden porch, noticing the empty potting soil bags and the freshly planted flowers, and took a step forward to look inside the open door. He was about to call out *hello*, when he noticed a woman lying on the floor with her hands over her eyes. He quickly retreated, but his foot hit one of the wooden planks leaning against the door and sent them all crashing to the floor with a loud clap.

Miranda let out a cry, scrambled to her feet, and put her hand to her chest. "Oh, my God!"

They began talking over one another as the man clumsily tried to stand the wood planks back against the door. "I'm so sorry – "

"You startled me!"

"I didn't mean – "

They stood looking at one another, then Miranda pointed towards him. "Are you – "

"William." He leaned forward and extended his hand. "William Priestly."

Miranda started to shake his hand, then rubbed her palms on her jeans first. "Miranda. I've been cleaning and I was just – " she motioned to the floor where she had been stretched out. "Resting. Ben said you weren't arriving until next week."

"Sorry, I took an earlier flight. I can come back later, if you'd like." He began to leave.

"No, no, that's quite all right."

"I spoke to your husband this morning and he suggested that I stop by this afternoon."

Miranda waved away his concern. "Really, it's quite all right. So you're interested in renting the garden house for the summer?"

"Perhaps for two months or so, if that's all right."

"That's fine. We don't have any plans for it at the moment. Come in, come in. I'll show you around." Miranda cleared some of the cleaning supplies out of the way and set them against the wall. "Well, here it is." She made a sweeping gesture with her arm. "Just one large room, for the most part."

William took a step inside, and let his eyes wander over the place.

"We fixed it up over the years, using it mostly for our kids' parties and sleepovers. But they're gone now, so we thought we'd try renting it out. Maybe make a few minor renovations."

She smiled and waited for him to walk around or ask questions, but he just stood there with his hands behind his back.

"Well, let me give you a quick tour. We're in the living room/bedroom/study," she said in a playful tone. As she looked at the double bed with its blue and rose bedcover and the assortment of pillows, it struck her as being perhaps too feminine.

One of her hand-painted floral screens and the dresser formed a kind of wall, offering some degree of privacy. But these, too, were draped with lace. "You can move anything that's in the way," she said, lifting a corner of the lace and letting it drop.

Against the wall stood a large desk and an overstuffed chair with a lamp behind it. William walked over and ran his hand across the desk. "Looks like oak."

"It is. A teacher's desk from the 1940s or so. I found it at a garage sale years ago." She showed him the sliding panel that pulled out. "For grading papers, I guess."

He smiled. "They don't make them like this anymore."

Miranda pointed to the other side of the room. "We might put up a wall there, divide it up a bit. We're not sure yet." She pointed to the wooden rafters up above. "High ceilings for such a small place."

Again, she waited for William to say something, but he just lifted his eyes to the ceiling.

"The kids had a Halloween party here one year — a kind of haunted house. Skeletons hanging from the rafters. A gauntlet of horrors — you know, blindfold the kids and dip their hands into cold, oily spaghetti." She lowered her voice and said, "These are the brains of Frankenstein. These are his eyes."

William waited for her to explain.

She laughed lightly. "Hard-boiled eggs. Anyway – back here is the bathroom." She opened the door and pointed to the shower. "Good water pressure."

"And over here is the kitchen. Small, but kind of cozy. And nice with the window right by the table." She parted the blue calico curtains and smiled at the view of branches arcing over the window. "That's a butterfly bush. It will bloom in a few more weeks. All purple. You might see some monarchs, or some of those yellow-and-black tiger butterflies."

"Very nice," William said.

"And there's a separate back entrance." She opened the French doors, revealing several flowering bushes and a gravel patch. "There's room to park back here and enter this way. Very private." Miranda felt her cheeks heat up, realizing that she had implied something she didn't intend. "Convenient for bringing in the groceries." She closed the doors, and moved back to the main room.

She pointed to a wall of cupboards and closets. "Lots of storage. I think the people we bought it from built all these. Or maybe someone before them. I don't really know." She opened and closed them as she spoke. "You can hang things in this one. There's still a lot of stuff in them from when the kids were young. Just move things around if you need the space."

"I don't have too much. It's all very comfortable." He noticed some steps along the wall and raised his head to see where they ended.

"A loft," said Miranda. "The steps are a little steep, and it gets hot up there in the summer. But it's nice to have the extra bed for visitors." She walked to the front door. "Well, that's pretty much it. What do you think? Will it suit you?"

"It's very nice. A real haven. I would love to rent it. Unless you have other people interested in it?"

"No, we never got around to advertising it. So it's yours if you like. I can have it ready by Saturday. Or tomorrow if you want."

"Saturday is fine. Thank you."

They walked out onto the low porch. Miranda scooped up the empty potting soil bags and stuffed them into some of the empty flower containers. "I can change the quilt, if you like."

William turned to Miranda, unsure of what she meant.

"I mean if it's too feminine. I have others if you'd prefer."

William smiled at her concern. "No. It's fine. It's all very comfortable. It feels – " he looked around for the words to describe it. "It feels like – a real home."

Miranda laughed. "It *is* a real home. An extension of the house." She gazed lovingly at the cottage. "A lot of happy memories here."

William stepped off the porch and looked at it from a few paces back, clearly admiring it. He noticed the small hand-painted sign above the door, and read, "The Forget-Me-Not House."

"My daughter named it that when she was little. But somehow we always refer to it as the Garden House."

"How many children do you have?"

"Two. Michael and Clara. They both moved away recently. Michael to his first job in Portland; he just graduated in engineering. And Clara moved to San Francisco. She lived at home while she went to college here, but when her boyfriend was transferred to San Francisco, she decided to switch schools and join him there." Miranda knew she would go on and on about the kids if she didn't stop herself. She stepped off the porch and shielded her eyes against the sun. "Are you from New York, William?"

"Pennsylvania, originally."

She nodded and waited for him to say more, but he remained silent. After a moment, she asked, "And Ben said you're a teacher?"

"Yes. I teach English."

"What level?"

"I teach at a community college. Composition and literature. Thought I'd use the summer to get some reading done. Work on a few journal articles. I think this place will be perfect for that." He shaded his eyes and looked over at the sloped landscape.

"Looks like you have quite a garden there." He began to walk back to the flagstone steps.

"Come this way," Miranda said, gesturing to her left. "We'll take the scenic route back. Through the garden."

The path she took led to a terraced landscaped area that winded up towards the house. Her pride was her garden and she wanted to see William's reaction to it. She knew it would be at its best; it had rained yesterday and was now luxuriating in the warm afternoon sun.

"You're lucky," she said. "We've had such a cool, late spring that many of the early flowers are still in bloom." A note of excitement filled her voice. Seeing her garden through other people's eyes always gave her a thrill, and a burst of gardening inspiration usually followed.

Miranda led the way to the lower garden, where the tree-like rhododendrons and lower azaleas formed a sort of double wall; a few purple, magenta, and white blooms still lingered on the bushes. She loved every section of her garden, but this shadier and damper part always stirred in her a feeling of tenderness. It grew thick with hosta and ferns, and perennials that didn't need much care – patches of bleeding hearts and shy lily-of-the-valley.

"Oh, look!" she cried. "The coral bells have bloomed." She bent down to take a closer look. "Clara always called these fairy flowers."

The perfume of the lily-of-the-valley pulled her closer to them; she picked a tiny sprig, and held it to her nose. Then she tucked it under her wedding band as a reminder to come back and gather a small bouquet of the shade flowers to show Ben.

Where the path began to climb, the garden widened, as if opening its arms in welcome. A slight breeze gently animated the garden, swaying the weeping willow branches, and causing low notes of wind chimes to fill the air. Filtered sunlight made its way through the tree branches, casting shadow and light among the plants. Miranda brushed her hand against a clump of pink astilbes, their feathery plumes illuminated by a shaft of light.

She gestured for William to take the lead up the tiered steps. Though she couldn't see his face, she could tell that he was taking it all in, pausing in front of some her favorite things: the wrought iron chair entwined with ivy, the birdhouses and birdbaths scattered throughout. He paused to look at the rustic benches and tables, the clusters of flowers. When they came upon the goldfish pond, he turned and smiled at her.

"My son and Ben made that for me one Mother's Day. And Ben added the little bridge a few years back. Ben's an architect, you know, and enjoys carpentry."

William stopped to run his hand over an old sundial, its base nestled in a cloud of cobalt blue lobelia. He seemed to enjoy spotting the almost hidden clay sculptures peeking out from clumps of flowers: winged figures, tiny houses, rabbits, birds. He stopped and looked back over the garden. "It's beautiful. Interesting."

Miranda smiled out at her garden, delighted that he understood. Over the years, she had shown it to many different people. Some of them loved it and felt at home in it – others were seemingly indifferent, or commented on the bother of weeding or the cost of upkeep, which let her know that they didn't really see it.

"Are you the gardener?" William asked. "Someone put a lot of thought into this, a lot of themselves."

"Oh, the whole family made it, really. Ben helps with the planting and trimming. He put in a sprinkler system two years ago, which really helped, and last year he added the antique iron fencing. Michael made some of the benches and tables. And Clara insisted on the swing," she said, gesturing to a wooden swing that hung from an oak tree, with faded blue ribbons tied at the seat.

William stood still and took it all in. "It's really remarkable. A sense of peace pervades it. I feel like I've stepped out of time."

"Feel free to use it anytime you want. There are several good reading spots. And there's a hammock down below that we put up every summer. Just brush away the pine needles and leaves."

They reached the sunny upper garden where a bubbling fountain stood among brightly colored blooms. Daisies, dahlias, and clumps of daylilies crowded against each other, and pressed against the benches, trellises, and fencing. With the afternoon breeze lightly swaying the plants, and small white butterflies darting from flower to flower, the garden appeared vibrant, joyful even.

As they strolled back to William's car, Miranda felt suddenly very happy. "It will be nice to have someone enjoying the garden house and garden. They don't get much attention anymore – not like they used to."

"I'm sure I'll enjoy them both." William extended his hand. "On Saturday, then. Around 10:00?"

"That'll be fine." She shook his hand and watched him get into his car and drive away. Then she went back down to close up the garden house and pick her bouquet, her spirits strangely lifted.

*

Miranda arrived at the restaurant a few minutes early and found a seat by the wall of windows. She ordered a glass of wine, and began to make a list of things to get done: organize the drawers and cupboards, clean out the garage, go through the closets – including her own. It had taken her half an hour to find something to wear for tonight. She had wanted to change her look a bit, but everything she tried on was too tight. So she had settled on the usual black skirt and her favorite blue sweater. But she wore her hair loose for a change, and put on a brighter shade of lipstick.

She brought her hand to one of her earrings, the lapis lazuli drops Clara gave her for her birthday, and remembered her comment: "You should dress up more often, Mom."

Clara was right. She needed updating. There were things in her closet she hadn't worn in over twenty years. She needed to get rid of things, start fresh. Though there were some pieces she just couldn't part with. Clothes that reminded her of her younger days, when all her life was before her.

She gazed out the window, remembering how she used to dress in velvets and satins, Victorian jewelry and long 1920s necklaces, vintage blouses and dresses. Everything Bohemian and dramatic, though it hadn't seemed so at the time.

She used to ride her bike to school in long skirts, dress up to visit galleries, and work at her various part-time jobs wearing clothes from vintage stores, consignment shops, and import stores – many of the shops located in the Pike Place Market. She remembered the thrill of adventure when she escaped her department store job and explored the Market over her lunch hour. Running down the stairs in Post Alley, and then wandering through the maze of stores, delighting in the Tibetan beads, the Moroccan vases, the antique lace collars, the incense and oils from far away. More often than not, the adventure ended with the purchase of a few pieces of rose-flavored Turkish Delight – the pale-pink, translucent candy dusted in powdered sugar came to symbolize the promise of future travel.

Miranda gave a deep sigh. Youth should be a time of hope and promise. She saw that in the kids now, especially in Clara. For the past several years, Clara's dreams had also been her dreams. She had convinced Clara to take two weeks in the summer to travel, before settling into her classes in the fall; and it was as if a part of her was making the trip as well.

Miranda looked down at her bullet points – cleaning out closets and drawers? That is one boring list, she thought, wadding it up.

Some part of her sat up and wondered why middle age, or any age for that matter, shouldn't also be a time of hope and promise. Why should youth be the only time of discovery? Why was that early dreaming self at odds with her current sense of self? She remembered the feeling of being all fired up by starting a new painting, whether it was a medieval miniature or a whimsical landscape, or experimenting with silk-screening, or learning how to use a potter's wheel.

But without the dreams that accompanied youth, such pursuits now seemed like dead ends.

Some vital connection was gone. Her garden, her home, her kids – that was her life. And those things had filled her, until recently. Had it been turning fifty? Or the fact that the kids had left home and moved away? Did she even have a purpose in life anymore?

She saw Ben enter the restaurant, and a feeling of happiness washed over her. His presence often served as ballast to her wandering thoughts that sometimes carried her too far away.

As he approached the table, she arched her eyebrows.

"I know, I know," he said, kissing her cheek and sitting next to her. "William called to say he was in town early and asked if he could stop by to see the place. I had the phone in my hand to call you, but I got interrupted, and then I was pulled into a meeting, and then – " He threw his hands up. "I didn't remember until I was almost here."

"A phone call would have been nice. I nearly jumped out of my skin when he appeared at the garden house."

Ben playfully nudged her, letting her know that he didn't buy her annoyance with him.

She leaned into him, and handed him a glass of wine. "I ordered it for you."

He took a sip, and let his gaze linger on Miranda. "You look great, Honey. What'd you do?"

"Flattery will get you nowhere," she said, though she was happy he noticed.

Ben took the menu she handed him, and opened it. "So, what did you think of Mr. William Priestly?"

Miranda gave a light shrug. "He seems like a nice guy. Quiet. I think he'll be a good tenant. He's young, Ben. I thought you said he was old."

"No, I said he was around thirty."

"No, you said he'd been teaching for thirty years."

"I didn't say that."

"Yes, you did. I expected a much older man. I had no idea who he was at first."

"Well, what do you think? Are you okay with having him as a tenant for the summer? Or do you want to set up your studio? Because I thought about it, and maybe it's time to make those changes. Put up that wall, if you want. Make the window bigger."

Miranda took a sip of wine and looked away. "I'm not quite ready yet for the studio. Fall will be soon enough."

They ordered their meals, and then she began to butter a piece of bread. "I'm actually kind of glad that the garden house will be used. It's such a pretty place. And William really seemed to appreciate the garden."

"Then he'll be the perfect tenant," laughed Ben. His phone rang and he frowned at the name. "Sorry, Honey. It's the Difficult client," he said, stepping away to take the call.

Miranda held the wine glass in her hand and gazed out the window. The sun was lowering in the west. A pair of Canadian geese glided onto the water, making long golden ripples that widened into dark lines flecked with shimmery pink and orange. I could paint that, she thought. Just the water. If only I could capture that ephemeral beauty, those fleeting shades of color and light.

Ben sat back down, shaking his head. "Now she wants the sunroom where the kitchen is, and she wants the kitchen – Oh, well. No need to talk about work now." He clasped Miranda's hand.

His warm hand brought her back into the moment. She gazed into his smiling eyes, and impulsively brought his hand to her lips and kissed it. "You make me happy, Ben."

He gave a start of mock surprise. "Is that the wine talking?"

She laughed. "Maybe it is. But you *do* make me happy. You always have."

Ben's face filled with pleasure and he squeezed her hand. "I hope so."

Chapter 3

~

One week later, Miranda had cleaned out several closets, the kitchen drawers and a few cupboards, and was now tackling the boxes in the garage. She filled a crate with some of her old pieces, torn between throwing them away and letting Paula look through them; but she had promised her. At worst they would gather dust in Paula's shops.

Miranda now had several bags of things to be donated, and a separate pile to be tossed. She placed four large shopping bags in the back of the car, and headed to the Salvation Army store.

As she drove, she realized that having a tenant didn't make a difference in her life at all. But then, why should it? Yet she was somewhat disappointed that William was seldom around, and when he was, he was on his computer or jotting down notes. Rather than being on a relaxing vacation, he was intensely busy. Should she try to talk to him? Find out why he kept to himself so much? She could almost hear Ben warning her: Don't interfere; how William spends his time is his business.

She suddenly remembered a homeless shelter she had come across a few weeks earlier while running last minute errands for Michael. She had gotten turned around and stumbled upon the shelter for teens. She wanted to find a good home for the things she had reluctantly parted with: some board games, a badminton set, a pair of skates that Clara had never really used, a small lamp, and some other odds and ends that she thought young people would enjoy.

Miranda circled several blocks before locating the shelter again. She parked across the street, scrutinizing the building before deciding to go in. It was more run down than she remembered.

She carried in two bags, passing a teenage girl working a pitiful little garden on the side of the building. On the second trip, Miranda saw that the girl was struggling with the hard soil; she dug a hole, put in a bushy plant, and then patted the soil around it. Miranda felt an immediate kinship with the young gardener, and walked over to her.

"Hi there! Starting a garden?"

When the young girl looked up, Miranda winced, noticing the bruised cheek and swollen lip.

The girl bristled at the expression of pity that filled Miranda's face.

Miranda quickly shifted her attention to the garden. "Oh – you've planted shade and sun flowers together." She pointed to the little bush the girl had just planted. "Bleeding hearts need protection. This would do much better over there, away from the sun."

The girl rose to her feet and appeared to be deeply offended, but she quickly covered it with a derisive laugh. She looked down at the bags in Miranda's hands. "Bringing us your rejects? Or did you just come here to give gardening advice?"

Miranda stood speechless. She had wanted to encourage and befriend the young girl. She was about to explain herself, but the girl's folded arms, raised chin, and narrowed eyes told Miranda to leave it alone. She picked up the bags and went inside.

"Rich bitch," she heard the young girl mutter.

Miranda whipped around, ready to set her straight – on both points. But the girl had thrown down her gardening tool and was walking away. With a stab of pity, Miranda saw that the tool was an old, bent spoon.

She walked inside, doubting her decision to come to this place. The building was gloomy and depressing in spite of the colorfully painted sign that hung over the entrance. As she opened the door, she was met with a flurry of activity and caught a whiff of vomit and pine-scented cleanser. A young girl was being helped away to a room. Raised voices came from down the hall. Miranda felt her stomach tighten, and she remained rooted to the floor.

A woman behind the counter was on the phone, but had noticed Miranda and now pointed to a sign on the wall that said *Donations*.

Miranda smiled her thanks and walked over to a large box. Except for candy wrappers, cigarette butts, and dust balls, the box was empty. She gently placed the bags inside, and offered a tentative smile to two sullen teens who slouched on a nearby bench.

The older boy pushed himself up, and began rummaging through the bags. As Miranda walked away, she heard him snort in amusement.

"Badminton?" he asked in disbelief. Then he and the other boy burst out laughing.

Mirada hurried down the steps and went straight to her car. As she drove off, she defended her intentions. She had only given items that were still in good shape; not rejects. And the badminton set was full of good memories from when the kids were young. She told herself that she was being overly sensitive. These were angry teenagers, runaways, perhaps abandoned, or even abused.

As she waited for the light to change, she briefly imagined the pierced and tattooed teens leaping in a lighthearted game of badminton – and had to laugh. What had she been thinking? Try as she might, she still did everything with her kids in mind, assuming that what they had liked, these other teens would, as well.

Clara and Michael had moved on, but she had not. There she was, cleaning their rooms, cooking and shopping for four, doing everything as if they might walk in the front door and ask what was for dinner.

Miranda spent the rest of the afternoon working in her garden, raking out the dead underbrush and carrying it down to the compost pile. She saw that the daylight was beginning to fade, and she felt unexpectedly overcome with weariness. A few drops of rain began to fall, making a muted patter as it landed on the leaves.

She walked over to the old swing and sat down on it, rocking back and forth, her hand playing with the faded satin bow that she had tied there for Clara so many years ago. When the knot holding the bow suddenly split apart, Miranda gave a little gasp and felt a fresh sense of loss. She let the soft rain and the darkening light make a kind of curtain around her. She sat in the swing until it was nearly dark, holding the bit of blue ribbon in her hand.

*

Ben kept glancing at Miranda over dinner. "Is everything all right? You seem tired."

"I've been dragging all day. I guess I didn't sleep well last night. Some dream kept me awake."

"About what?"

She searched her mind, then lifted her shoulders. "I can't remember."

Ben gave her a few moments to say more, but she remained silent. "Looks like you made some progress on the garage. You finally throwing out that bag of broken dishes?"

"No. I'm finally going to use them." She waited for him to comment on how many years the bag had been sitting in the garage.

But Ben just wanted to get her to talk, so that he could find out what was bothering her. "Did you get rid of a lot of stuff?"

"I threw away a lot. Gave a couple of things to Paula. And I dropped off some bags at a shelter for teens. It was – upsetting. To see these young kids – bruised, defensive, hurt." She shook her head at the memory. "And angry. One girl was really rude to me."

"Maybe you should stick to the Salvation Army."

"I suppose so." Miranda took another helping of salad and tried to sound even-toned, cheerful even. "I spoke to Clara today."

Ben looked up. Aha. Here it was. "And?"

"She's changed her mind about traveling this summer. Wants to get started with classes instead."

"Oh, well. She can always go later."

Miranda took a moment before answering. "I don't think she'll be going anytime soon. She's made up her mind – she's going to study Law."

"What happened to Comparative Literature?"

"She said that was what *I* wanted, not her. I never pushed her in that direction."

"Not pushed, maybe," said Ben, "but strongly encouraged."

"Because I thought that was what she wanted."

"Well, Law was her original choice, after all."

They ate in silence for a few minutes. Miranda pushed around the lettuce leaves on her plate, and then set her fork down.

"I would have given anything for the chance to tour the Lake District," she finally said. "To explore London and Paris, visit Monet's garden." Those dreams still loomed large in Miranda's mind. "I just don't understand it."

"That's because *you* love that sort of thing. She has other interests. She has to do what's right for her."

"I know. It's just that…" Miranda left the sentence unfinished. She couldn't help feeling that it was her dream being crushed by Clara's decision.

She started to clear the table. "Do you want coffee?"

"Are you going to have some?"

She considered it, then shook her head. "I don't think so. I think I'll just go up and take a bath."

He reached over and rubbed her shoulder. "Go on. I'll clean up here."

She went upstairs, and ran the bath water. Then she reached for the lilac sea salts and poured them into the bath, swishing her hand around the water to make them dissolve faster. She straightened up, and placed her hands on her lower back, looking into the water.

She wasn't herself, she thought. It was more than just Clara's decision. For the past few days she felt that something was nagging at her, nudging her. But she couldn't detect the source of the unease. It was as if something were tapping her on the shoulder, asking her to pay attention. She used to get that feeling when something was wrong with one of the kids. Maybe she had sensed Clara's change of heart. Ben would laugh at that. He always ridiculed her vague intimations, her belief that she often picked up on other people's feelings.

A hot bath would help. She stepped into the fragrant water and sighed as the tension and fatigue gradually left her muscles. Her nightly bath had become a ritual. A leftover from her waitressing days – a way to wash off the workday, and welcome the night. Part of the ritual was to turn off the overhead light and allow the room to be illuminated by the gold filigree nightlight. As soft as candlelight.

She pulled the shower curtain across the bath, sealing in the steam. That final gesture always signified a sinking into a world of calm, of honoring the end of the day, and marking the beginning of night.

As she adjusted to the prickling hot water, she sank deeper into the bath. She gave another sigh of relaxation, held her breath, and slid under the water, shaking out her hair, aware only of the water, the holding of her breath.

Then with a splash, she sat up, flashing on her dream from the night before. Her face filled with worry, seeing the vivid details.

Sunlight on water as she swam in a pool, the sense of well-being, children's laughter nearby. Then, deeper into her dream, she heard a dog's whimper. It seemed to come from a vent in the pool wall. She swam closer and looked inside.

A dark, earthen chamber came into focus and she caught a glint of something. She peered closer, and when her eyes adjusted to the darkness, she saw that it was the metal frame of glasses on a man. He sat cross-legged in the darkness, next to a muzzled dog.

A voice said, "That's Jasper." With a rush of revulsion, Miranda realized he had been watching her swim.

She pushed off from the pool wall and tried to run away, but the water was resistant, slowing her. She gathered the children from the shallow end, and hurried them out of the pool, casting a wary glance behind her.

With a shudder, she tried to puzzle out the meaning of the dream. Who was the man sitting in the dark place – was he watching her, or the children? Why was the dog muzzled, and why was it whimpering?

She tried to find any significance in the images. A childhood friend had a dog named Jasper, who used to wait for them outside the public pool. But the feeling from the dream was that it was the man's name. She used to take the kids swimming, but why dream of that now? Or did those memories have nothing to do with the dream?

Miranda instinctively reached for the bar of soap, as if she could cleanse away the disturbing image. She usually had good dreams. Where had this one come from? Was she worried about Michael and Clara? She couldn't pinpoint the emotion of the dream – something akin to apprehension, dread, the need to protect. She shook off the feeling. It was just a dream, after all.

She finished her bath, dried her hair, and put on her fleece pants and sweatshirt. The Seattle nights were still cool, especially with the light rain that continued to fall. She went downstairs.

Ben was at his desk, working on the layout for a cabin he planned to someday build near Sam's. Just a small weekend place.

Miranda leaned over and wrapped her arms around him as he explained the drawing of the deck.

"An outdoor fireplace? I like that. It would feel like another room."

"With a partial overhang," he said, sketching in the detail.

"Sounds nice."

"We could even have a hot tub out there – wouldn't that feel great?" he asked.

She gave him a light squeeze, and went to the window. She parted the curtains and saw that a heavier rain was now falling. Down below in the garden house, a yellow light shone through the window. She was used to it being dark at night. It now appeared warm, welcoming, reminding her of when the kids used it.

"It's nice, isn't it – the garden house being used?" she said, more as a comment than a question. She continued to watch the lighted window, squinting ever so slightly. "Do we know any Jaspers?"

"Jaspers?" Ben asked, turning around. "I don't think so. Why?"

"Just a strange dream I had." She rubbed her arms, and remained looking out into the darkness. She was about to close the curtain, when she saw William appear in the garden house window. He gazed out at the rain for a few moments, then took something from his wallet and looked at it. A photo, or perhaps a business card. Then he returned it to his wallet, and closed the blinds.

"We really don't know anything about him, do we?" Miranda asked.

"Who?" Ben saw that she was still looking down at the garden house. "William? What do you mean?"

Miranda gave a tiny shrug. "Letting a complete stranger into your home. It's kind of an odd thing to do."

"Well, we didn't do a background check or anything. But a personal recommendation is always best. Don't you think?"

"Yes," Miranda said, and let the curtain fall.

Chapter 4

~

Miranda hung up the phone, and went upstairs. She threw the towels and clothes into the laundry basket, more upset by Clara's words than she wanted to admit: "Just because you gave up your dreams, Mom, doesn't mean I'm going to give up mine. I'm sure about David, and I'm sure about Law." Meaning that Miranda had never finished her degree, or pursued her art.

But how could she have? There was always something preventing her. In the early years of her marriage, she kept at her painting and sculpting, and began to explore gardening and cooking, with the same energy and passion to create. But little by little, she had put her things away. Focused on the kids. Was happy doing so, but now that they were gone, she was left with a void and felt disconnected from that earlier sense of self.

As she walked down the hall, she paused in front of the framed photos on the wall. Michael's graduation picture. Another of him and Clara as teenagers at Multnomah Falls. Ben helping them find sea glass at the beach when they were little. Clara looking up from her stroller with her small face full of wonder.

Miranda set the laundry basket down, and went into Clara's room. She fluffed the pillows on the bed, and straightened the items on the dresser. The room felt so empty and quiet. She walked over to the bookshelves, lifted down the Heidi doll, and sat on the bed. It was almost a month since the kids moved away. She had known that she would miss them, but she wasn't prepared for the emptiness that now filled her.

She returned the doll to the shelf, and left the room.

In the laundry room, she began to separate the clothes into dark and light. She put the towels in, and was about to add detergent, but stopped – the black void of the washing machine seemed to widen and spread as she stared into it.

I need to get out, she thought. This can wait.

Miranda put on her shoes, grabbed her keys, and left the house, with the intention of walking off the growing darkness inside her. She left in such a hurry that she didn't notice Paula waving from her driveway.

Paula held a bag of groceries in her arms and called out. "Hey! Where are you off to in such a hurry?"

Miranda stopped, and crossed over to the fence. "Oh – I didn't see you. I thought I'd get some air. Go on a walk."

"You okay?" Paula never missed a thing.

"Just having one of those mornings," Miranda said, trying to make light of it.

"What happened?" Paula asked.

"Oh, nothing, really. Just missing the kids, not sleeping well, weird dreams." As soon as she said it, she wished she hadn't. Paula loved analyzing dreams.

"What kind of dreams?"

"I hardly remember – just fragments. Swimming in a pool. Kids. Some weirdo watching."

Paula nodded, as if figuring it out. "That's your subconscious mind processing what Nicole said about the daycare."

Miranda quickly forgot her problems. "I haven't seen her – what did she say? Did something happen?"

"Oh, little Danny came home saying a man was trying to take away his best friend. But I saw one of the teachers at the store and she didn't know anything about it. Just one of his tall tales."

Miranda looked down at the ground, her brow contracted. She hated all the stories of abductions and abuse that seemed to be part of the daily news.

"I remember having troubling dreams when my kids left home," said Paula. "It's normal. You miss the kids, you're worried about them, but you can't do anything about it, so you have nightmares."

Miranda nodded. "I'm sure that's it."

"How's the tenant working out? Are you happy with your decision?"

"Oh, fine, fine. We don't see much of him." She looked in the direction of the garden house, but didn't add anything more.

"Well, I need to put these things away. Listen Miranda, it can take a while to find your stride, but let me tell you – once you do, you'll love it. You'll finally get around to all the things you've been wanting to do."

"Like getting into shape," Miranda said, straightening up and smiling. "I'm sure you're right about everything. A walk will do me good." She waved goodbye and picked up her pace.

She breathed deeply, inhaling the cool morning air. It felt good to walk, to get her body moving. She wondered when, and why, she had stopped making exercise a part of her life. She had always taken the kids swimming and on walks, and she and Ben had always hiked and camped around the Northwest. Things had a way of just slipping away.

Miranda's spirits improved as she walked higher and higher up the hill, taking in the gardens, the pretty homes, the view of Lake Washington.

She had to stop once or twice to catch her breath, and she could feel the burn in her calves. I've gotten so out of shape, she thought. Soft. This is exactly what I need – to push myself more, expect more of myself, to wake up and get moving – with everything. Paula's right. This is a new beginning to be embraced.

But when she turned the corner, she was pulled right back into worry. A pool maintenance truck was driving off. Once again, the creepiness of the swimming dream filled her. She knew the dream was exactly what Paula said it was – a mom dream, and maybe an unconscious nagging to get back into shape, mixed with the memory of her friend's dog, Jasper. Dreams rarely made sense. And yet.

Though she didn't understand how, she knew the dream was connected to her recent sense of unease. But unease about what, she couldn't say. It was like trying to catch an image at the far periphery of vision.

She wanted to see where the pool was. Who owned it. She crossed to where the truck had pulled out, and stood near the shoulder-high laurel bushes that surrounded a backyard. She moved to a spot where the bushes were not so thick, and peeked over the top. On the side of the house was a swimming pool, smooth and blue in the morning light. She paused indecisively, and then pushed aside the branches and stepped through, to take a better look.

"May I help you?"

Miranda jumped. She hadn't seen anyone and was startled to realize that she wasn't alone. A woman, perhaps in her late sixties or so, stood before an easel with a paintbrush poised in one hand.

"Oh, good morning," said Miranda. "Sorry – I didn't mean to intrude. I just wanted to get a better look at your pool. I saw the maintenance truck drive away. I'm thinking of getting one. A pool, that is."

"Hmm," said the woman, for the most part ignoring Miranda's rambling explanation. She studied the canvas, dabbed at her palette, and made a few strokes. "Well, it's certainly good exercise."

Miranda saw that she was painting a grouping of potted flowers. "I used to paint," she volunteered. "A little."

"Did you? And why did you stop?"

"I forget. I mean, well, I still do. Sometimes. I plan on starting again."

"You should. It's a nice way to connect with the world, isn't it?" The woman lifted a glass from a small table next to her, took a sip, and set the glass back down.

With a few blinks of surprise, Miranda realized that it was a glass of champagne. How wonderfully eccentric! She looked more closely at the woman. She was strikingly beautiful, with wavy gray hair down to her shoulders, and though she wore a long blue caftan, Miranda saw that her arms were well toned and that she was in good shape. She probably swam every morning. A large table with comfortable chairs around it stood next to the house, as if ready for summer gatherings. The entire pool area was full of flowers, climbing vines, and wicker chairs with colorful pillows.

"How pretty you've made everything!"

The woman gave an appreciative smile to Miranda, and then swished the brush around in a jar of water.

Miranda was about to leave, when she heard a tiny yelp. At the woman's feet lay a small dog, its tail thumping languidly.

Miranda bit her lip, unsure about pushing on. "You know, I think I've seen you and your husband in the neighborhood." Miranda made some vague gestures. "About this tall, wears glasses, I think."

"My husband and I parted ways years ago," the woman said, deciding on another color from her palette.

"Oh, gosh. I'm sorry."

"I'm not," the woman said, taking a sip of champagne. "It's much better this way."

Miranda opened her mouth as if to say something, but then took a step back. "Well, goodbye. Enjoy your morning."

"Yes, I intend to." The woman raised her head in goodbye. "I hope you get your pool."

Miranda stepped back into the street, with two thoughts foremost in her mind. One, that she had just carried out the most pathetic act of sleuthing imaginable. And two, she felt inspired by the older woman.

She walked back down the hill, trying to remember where she had packed away her free weights. It was time to get them out again, time to become physically stronger. Would she ever exude such calm confidence as the woman by the pool? Miranda wondered if that was the kind of freedom older women sometimes referred to – the freedom to speak your mind, to do what you want when you want, to behave the way you want. She thought of the long blue caftan, the tanned arms, the champagne!

Though such an image intrigued her, she didn't think she could ever be so self-contained. She would always want Ben and the kids by her side, or at least close by. Still, she wondered what it would be like to enjoy that kind of ease – to be so comfortable in her own skin. What would happen if she dressed the way she wanted to, and spoke her mind, and created whatever she wanted to? She thrilled at the possibility that inside her was another woman, just waiting to come into being.

In a burst of inspiration, she decided she would make a special dinner for Ben out on the deck. And wear something pretty for a change. Why shouldn't every day be special? Maybe her life would never involve grand occasions and exotic destinations, but she could at least make her day-to-day life as wonderful as possible. Like she used to. How had she forgotten about that?

When Miranda arrived home, she showered and then began to rummage through the cupboard under the stairs. Yet more stuff to be gone through. In one box she found her old art supplies. She lifted some of the tubes of pigment, wondering if they were still good. She doubted it. But the brushes were fine. After staring at the contents for a few moments, she closed up the box, but moved it to the front of the cupboard. Then, after going through several more boxes, she found her hand weights and set them out.

She cleared a corner of the living room for floor exercises, and placed the weights there. Then she glanced at the time, surprised that it had gotten so late, and realized that she wouldn't have time to make anything too elaborate for dinner. Besides, something light and fresh sounded more appealing. She decided on a few appetizers to enjoy out on the deck, and later they could have salad and sautéed fish.

Miranda spent the rest of the afternoon making two different dips, preparing savory puff pastries, and marinating some salmon for later. As ideas came to her, she added them to a new list: morning walks, tone arms, 50 sit-ups a day, clean out her closet and buy some new clothes. Go back to school? Start painting? Look into buying a small kiln?

She called Ben and asked him to pick up some wine on his way home. When he asked why, she just laughed and said, "Because it's Friday. I thought we could sit out on the deck."

The deck was one of her favorite places to be in the long summer evenings. It was high off the ground and overlooked the garden house and back garden. One end was shaded by a pergola that dripped with wisteria in the early spring, and was now planted with climbing pink mandevillas. Pots of brightly colored fuchsias, and delicately scented carnations lined the deck; hanging geraniums and yellow thousand-bells draped over the railing. In the sun stood several pots of herbs for her cooking: rosemary, thyme, sage, and basil. The table and chairs were arranged close to the sliding glass door, and two chaise lounges with pillows faced out from the house – perfect for star gazing on clear nights.

Miranda took out one of her vintage table cloths, a floral one in blues and green and pale yellow. Then she went to the garden and snipped some white daisies and blue delphiniums and put them in a green earthenware jar for the middle of the table.

Soon, her blue crockery held vegetables, cheese, and the dips. She took a moment to admire how pretty it all looked. Then she ran upstairs, took off her t-shirt, and pulled on a pretty embroidered tunic and some gold hoop earrings. She started to put on a pair of sandals, then kicked them off. She loved being barefoot.

She went back to the deck and began to set the table. The phone rang just as she heard Ben come in the front door. After a few minutes, he slid open the screen door, with the phone cradled under his chin. He nodded and laughed into the phone. "Sounds like a plan. Here's your mom."

Miranda's face brightened, as it always did when the kids called. "Hi, Michael!" She listened with a big smile, by turns making sounds of surprise, agreement, and disbelief. She covered the phone and whispered to Ben, "There's a basket on the counter – bread and crackers."

Ben returned with the basket and poured them each a glass of wine.

Miranda touched her glass to Ben's, and motioned for him to taste the dips; she watched him try several, and was gratified by his obvious enjoyment of them. She said goodbye to Michael and set the phone down on the table.

"He sounds so happy. He wants us to bring his tent the next time we visit. I told him we could come next weekend, but he and some friends are going down to Crater Lake."

"Maybe the following week." Ben tried the puff pastry, took a sip of wine, and let out a deep sigh of relaxed pleasure. "What a great way to begin the weekend. We haven't done this for a while."

"I was thinking the same thing. But now that summer has arrived, we can be out here more."

They heard William drive by, and then saw him park his car behind the garden house. Miranda gave Ben a light shove. "Go see if he wants to join us."

"Oh, I don't know, maybe – "

"Go on, Ben. We never see him. We should make sure he's comfortable. He must be lonely, all by himself, working all the time."

"Maybe that's what he wants. If he wanted people around I guess he would have stayed home."

She gave him another push. "Go on. Just ask."

Miranda followed Ben to the deck stairs, and leaned against the railing as he walked down the path. She heard him call out, "Evening, William!"

William raised his head in greeting, and walked up to meet Ben. They exchanged a few words, with Ben pointing to the house, and then made their way towards the deck.

"Oh, good," said Miranda, and she stepped inside to get another place setting.

As they climbed the deck stairs, Miranda pulled out a chair at the table.

"Hi, William. Have a seat. Help yourself."

Ben poured out a glass of wine for William and set it in front of him.

William sat down and lifted his glass to them, and took a sip. "Thank you."

"I haven't seen you much to ask how you're doing," said Miranda." Are you comfortable? Is there anything you need?"

"I'm very comfortable. It's the perfect place to relax and get some work done."

"How's the reading and writing going?" Miranda asked, pushing the dishes of food in front of him.

"I'm getting a lot done, thanks to the park and the peacefulness of the garden. Every place seems conducive to writing." William looked around at the deck, taking in the comfortable mismatched furniture, more clay sculptures like the ones in the garden, the climbing vines and potted flowers. "What a nice arrangement you have out here."

Ben put a hand on Miranda's shoulder. "That's Miranda's doing. I built the deck, but she made it into this. She can transform any space into a little paradise."

Miranda frowned at Ben's praise. "Oh, it's just stuff I pull together. And flowers make anyplace pretty."

"No," insisted Ben. "Miranda has a knack for making a space beautiful and comfortable. She's a real artist."

William took a sip of wine and sank back into the cushioned chair. "I have to agree with Ben. Something about this space is very peaceful. Relaxing. Like the garden house, and the garden."

"I'm glad you like it," said Miranda. "We spend a lot of time out here in the summer. We grilled out here almost every weekend when the kids were here, didn't we Ben?"

"Even in the rain," laughed Ben.

Miranda scooted one of the dips closer to William. "Try this one. Artichoke and parmesan."

He took a cracker and tried the dip. Then indicated that it was indeed good, and took another.

"And she's quite a cook," added Ben.

Miranda shot Ben a look to stop with the compliments. It sounded too much like she was in need of praise.

"How long since your children moved away?" asked William.

"Just about a month," said Ben. "We're still getting used to it. For the most part they lived at home while they were in school. Then Michael found a job in Portland, and a week or so after that, our daughter, Clara, moved to San Francisco. At least they're not too far away."

"Though I wish they were closer," said Miranda.

Ben rubbed Miranda's shoulder. "It's been quite an adjustment for her."

"Oh, Ben," she said, shaking off his hand. "You miss them just as much as I do." There he was again, making her sound needy.

William nodded sympathetically. "That'll take some getting used to. But it must be gratifying to know that they're off to a good start in life."

Miranda smiled. "We're so proud of them. I thought Clara might study art and literature, she's always loved them so much. But she's decided to study Law. A solid, practical choice."

Ben jerked his head back in surprise and looked over at Miranda.

But she had run to the railing on hearing Paula call out to her. "Oh, look! Here's Paula and Derek." She turned to William. "Our neighbors. I've been wanting you to meet them."

Miranda welcomed them as they came up the deck stairs. "Hello! Come meet William! Can you join us?" She noticed that Paula was carrying a book.

"No," said Paula, "just a quick hello before we start out on our walk."

Miranda turned to Ben, knowing that Paula and Derek never turned down her cooking. But he had anticipated her. "More plates," he said, ducking inside.

William stood and smiled at the newcomers.

"This is William Priestly. He's a teacher from New York. These are our neighbors, Paula and Derek Morgan. They live just across from us."

"Welcome to the neighborhood!" said Paula. "Glad to finally meet you."

Derek shook William's hand. "I hear you'll be staying the summer. You'll love it here. Great neighborhood. Great neighbors," he added, grinning. "Have you been to the park yet, on the lake?"

"I have," said William. "Several times already."

"Have a seat," said Miranda. "You have to try these dips. Roasted pepper, and artichoke. Tell me what you think. And try this puff pastry – mushroom, onion, and gruyere."

Paula bit into the puff pastry, and closed her eyes with a sigh of enjoyment. She then tried the dips.

Ben slid open the screen door, and Miranda took the plates from him and set them on the table.

"Hey, buddy," said Ben, as Derek slapped him on the back. "How about a glass of wine? Or a cold beer?"

"Don't tempt us," answered Paula. She dipped another cracker into the roasted pepper dip. "This is week two of our walking program. We're determined this time. Mmm. This is just delicious, Miranda."

"Actually, a beer sounds great," said Derek.

"Derek!" cried Paula. Then she called out after Ben, "Make that two!" She fixed another cracker and gave it to Derek, and then turned to William. "So, Miranda says you're a teacher?"

"Yes. I'm using my summer vacation to get some research done."

"And writing articles," added Miranda.

"That too," said William.

"What brings you to Seattle?" asked Derek, taking the beer from Ben, and leaning against the deck railing.

"He knows someone at Ben's office," Miranda answered.

"I don't really know him," William said. "But someone I work with knows someone Ben works with."

"You mean you don't know anyone here?" asked Paula.

He shook his head. "But I've always heard that Seattle is nice. And every summer I try to see someplace new. Stay a month or so. I find it's the best way to get a feel for a place."

Miranda turned to Ben. "We should do that, Ben. Doesn't that sound like fun? I've always wanted to see Santa Fe, New Orleans – "

"Are you married? Any children?" asked Paula, going back to the artichoke dip.

William laughed a little. "No. Neither."

"Divorced?"

"Paula! Let him enjoy his food." Miranda felt protective of their new tenant and his quiet ways.

But William just smiled and didn't seem to mind. "No, that's okay. I guess you could say I'm married to my job."

Derek nodded. "I know how that is."

"Or the right person just hasn't come along," Paula said.

Miranda had been trying to kick Paula under the table, but kept getting Ben. He frowned at her, annoyed that he didn't know what she meant.

As they talked about their jobs, Paula leaned over to Miranda and handed her the book. "For you." She pointed to the subtitle, reading it out loud: "Attracting the Life You Want." Then she pulled a brochure from inside the book and handed it to Miranda. "And this."

Miranda read the heading of the seminar: *Starting a Small Business and Working from Home.*

"Oh. Thanks."

"Don't you want to know why I'm suggesting this?"

Miranda shrugged. "As a kick in the pants? To get me to stop talking about it, and start making things again?"

Paula slid out a white envelope from the book and handed it to her. "I sold two of your small flower paintings and the mosaic planter."

"You're kidding!" Miranda lit up at the news and tugged on Ben's sleeve. "Ben! Paula sold some of those things I gave her. Can you believe it?" She didn't wait for a response, but opened the envelope. "I can't take this, Paula! I was going to throw those things out."

Paula rolled her eyes and shoved the book to Miranda. "That's why you need to *read* this, and *go* to that," she said, pointing to the brochure.

Miranda shook her head in disbelief, then she counted out half the money. "Fifty percent for you?"

"Twenty – and I already took the shop's cut."

"You mean, this is *after*?" Miranda stared at Paula with her mouth open. "I did those so long ago. I can't believe anyone was interested."

"I told you they would sell. I had doubts about the planter – but I think mosaics are becoming popular again. You need to keep making things and figure out costs. I'll bring your pieces to the shops, and we'll see what happens. But I want to see some new stuff, too."

Miranda nodded in thought.

"And take a look at these," Paula said, tapping the book and brochure.

"I will. Though I'm not sure about the business part of it," she said, skeptically eyeing the brochure.

Paula tapped the envelope with the money in it. "*This* is the business part of it. Anyway, give it some thought." She took one last puff pastry, and then headed over to the stairs. "C'mon, Derek. We better go while it's still light. Nice meeting you, William."

Miranda leaned over the railing and called after them. "How about dinner soon? I want to try out a new recipe on you. Moussaka!"

"Just say when," answered Paula.

"The sooner, the better," added Derek. He threw his hands up at Paula who was already swinging her elbows in a brisk stride, and hurried to catch up with her.

Miranda smiled and waved, and then sat back at the table. "They're my guinea pigs. I try out new recipes on them."

"We've been neighbors for years," Ben added. "Our kids grew up together."

William listened as Ben and Miranda related different stories about them and the other neighbors, who was new, who had lived there before them, who had kids. William nodded and asked a few questions about the area.

After a while, he gazed up at the darkening sky and put his hands on his knees. "I guess I should be going. Organize my notes while they're still fresh in my mind." He stood and smiled at them both. "Thanks for the wine, and the appetizers were delicious."

Miranda beamed at the compliment, knowing they had turned out well.

"Any time, buddy," said Ben, rising to his feet.

"I'm so glad you came," said Miranda, "and that you got to meet Paula and Derek. Feel free to stop by any time you see us sitting out here. And just let me know if you need anything," she added, as he walked down the steps.

"I will, thank you. Goodnight."

Miranda watched him disappear into the dusk and make his way to the garden house.

Then she sat back at the table and threw her legs over Ben's lap. "That was nice, wasn't it? Having everyone here."

Ben gathered her legs closer to him. "Very nice."

"William seemed to enjoy himself." Miranda reached for her glass. "You don't think he was offended by Paula's questions, do you?"

"Nah. He seems like an easy going kind of guy."

Miranda handed the envelope to Ben. "Can you believe this?"

"Yes, I can. I've always told you that your work would sell."

"Well, it took me by surprise. And that they sold so quickly!" She leaned her head back in the chair and looked around at the deck. "William's right. It *is* nice here."

"I tell you that all the time, too," said Ben, "but it always matters more to you when you hear it from someone else."

"That's not true. But it's nice when someone else notices."

Chapter 5

~

Miranda sat on the floor in Clara's bedroom sorting through a pile of clothes that Clara claimed she no longer wanted. But Miranda was afraid that Clara had decided too impulsively and might change her mind about some of them. So she emptied the bags in the middle of the rug and was now going through them.

She soon realized that Clara had been right; most of the clothes were too small or too worn. But a few pieces were still in perfect condition, and one jacket still had the tags on it. Miranda briefly considered the girl at the shelter – she would be the right size. Then she shook her head. She didn't want to go back there.

She remembered the shifting expressions on the girl's face: vulnerability, anger, sarcasm. She must be about five years younger than Clara,

Miranda thought. She wondered what kind of a life the girl had lived, who had hurt her, what she was going to do.

Miranda set aside the best clothes and decided that she would, after all, take them to the shelter, along with a couple of shirts and pants that Michael no longer wanted. Perhaps the teens there might be able to use them.

She started to refold the clothes. As she leaned forward to pick up a sweater near the skirt of the bed, fragments of a dream from the night before came to her. She remembered that some sound had woken her from sleep. *Johnny!* someone had cried. Or had she dreamed it? She sat back, trying to remember the details. It was another disturbing dream.

A little boy. Quickly hiding beneath a bed as he heard the front door close. Slow, deliberate footsteps coming up the stairs. Terrified, the boy scooted back, pressed against the wall. He saw the man's shoes enter the room, stand in the doorway, and then leave.

Miranda stared at the bed skirt for a few seconds, then she leaned forward, lifted it, and peered beneath. Of course, there was nothing there. But why did she have such a dream? She wanted to get away from the unsettling images in her mind; she wanted to be outside, in her garden. She quickly finished folding and bagging the clothes, and took them downstairs.

She set the bags on the bench outside the front door, and turned on the hose. She watered the potted plants by the bench, and then watered the roses and blue star creeper that grew alongside the entrance to the house.

Being outside always dispelled any dark thoughts and gave her a sense of well-being. But as she stared at the beads of water on the pink petals and dark serrated leaves, a shadow filled her on remembering other images from recent dreams: a look of fear on the boy's face as a man's hand stroked his hair; a cigarette being put out on a small hand; someone wrapping protective arms around the boy. It seemed to be the same little boy in all the dreams. What was going on inside her that was causing such unwanted visions?

She shuddered at the images, and brushed at the water that had sprayed onto her legs. It was unlike her to have such troubling dreams. Surely it couldn't be from one visit to a shelter.

Miranda moved the hose to another bush, and remembered the times when she had such dreams before, usually about the kids. The time when Michael went to camp for the first time. The time in high school when Clara was in a relationship with an older, possessive boy. There had even been dreams about their friends, involving problems at school or at home. Though there wasn't much she could do, she had offered what support and advice she could.

Even though Ben discounted the dreams, she had known that the children were in need. And now she was getting the same kind of feeling, though it was hard to decipher – she couldn't separate her feelings at missing the kids from the dream feelings. And to add to it, she had to admit that what Paula said about the daycare had stuck in her mind. Danny was an imaginative child, but still, what if there was some truth to the story? Children sometimes picked up on things that adults didn't. What if there was a predator lurking around the neighborhood?

Ben's car pulled up and Miranda realized that she had completely drenched the rose bush. She moved the hose down to the next bush, and smiled over at Ben as he got out of the car.

He walked up to her, gave her a quick kiss, and set his jacket and briefcase on the bench next to the bags of clothing. "These going to the Salvation Army?" he asked, rolling up his sleeves.

"I'm going to take them to the shelter. I meant to put them in the car."

"Sure you want to go back there?" Ben reached for the hose and took over the watering, something he always enjoyed. "I thought you said the place was giving you nightmares."

"I didn't say that. I just said that I've been having weird dreams."

"Ever since you went there."

"I don't think the dreams have anything to do with the shelter." She uncuffed her pants and sat on the bench.

"Then why else are you having them?"

"Paula said she had such dreams each time one of her kids left home. Besides, I'm not going to be cowed by a few teenagers. They just don't know how to express things like anger and frustration. I've been through that with the kids." She looked through the bag closest to her. "Some of these clothes are like new."

Ben glanced at Miranda and then moved to water the plants on the other side of the sidewalk. Miranda jumped up to unloosen a kink in the hose, and then wiped her hands on her pants.

"There was one girl there, trying to make a little garden. She seemed so angry. It reminded me of that stage with Clara when everything I did made her so mad. Do you remember?"

"Just one of those phases," he said. "Kids can be moody. Growing pains, I guess."

Miranda considered this, remembering her own teenage years. For the most part, they had been good. She didn't remember being moody or unhappy. Though there were other girls who had seemed troubled. She vaguely remembered one girl from –

"I saw William as I drove past the park. Down by the playground. Looked like he had his laptop with him. He's not around much, is he?"

Miranda shook her head and bent over the rose bushes. "He comes and goes." She pulled off several brown petals and let them drop to the ground, next to the bright pink ones that had fallen off while being watered.

"Anything else need watering?" Ben turned to Miranda for an answer but she was staring down at the petals. "Honey? Miranda?"

She looked up. "Hmm? The ones by the trellis."

"What is it?"

Her forehead creased. "I was just remembering something. There was a girl in my class. In grade school, back when we lived in Oregon. Leanne. No, Liana. At first she went by Lee. But later she said that her true name was Liana, and asked us to call her that. Her family was new to town. She was an only child. For a while we were friends, four or five of us. There was something different about her. A distance she kept."

Miranda squinted into the past, trying to remember the shadowy girl. "She used to show us bruises and marks and told us that her father beat her. Once, she said that he did other things. None of us knew what she meant by that – or if any of it was true. She used to make up things. Said she had a beautiful twin sister who lived with a rich family, and that her real father was a famous scientist."

Miranda was silent for a few moments. "I think we were afraid to talk about it. Things weren't discussed openly like they are now. So many children are at the mercy of horrible people. Trapped."

"What made you think of her?" Ben pulled on the hose and began watering the hanging baskets by the door.

"I don't know. What if she was telling the truth? What if she was being abused and was hoping we could help?"

"What happened to her?"

Miranda looked out, trying to remember, then shook her head. "One day they were just gone. Moved away to somewhere else. I wish – I wish I would have done something. Told someone."

"I think you're more upset about that shelter than you realize. I wish you'd listen to me, Miranda, and not go back there."

"That's not it." Miranda frowned and plucked off a few more brown petals. "I think these roses could use some plant food."

As Ben jerked on the hose to gain more slack, Miranda saw that the hose pressed against one of the rose bushes, bending it. She rushed over to pull it away.

Chapter 6

Miranda pulled across from the shelter and unloaded the bags of clothing. It had been two weeks since she had first gone there. As she neared the front steps, she noticed a large pile of pulled weeds on the sidewalk and saw that the garden had been freshly edged and watered. She was surprised to see that the little bleeding heart had been moved to the shade and now had several delicate buds hanging from the stems. I can't believe the girl actually listened to me, she thought.

Miranda dropped off the bags inside in the donations box, and left. Coming around the corner, she almost collided with the same two boys from the first time, who were clearly surprised to see her again.

"Badminton, anyone?" she asked cheerfully.

As she drove off, she saw the young girl in her rear-view mirror. She was walking towards the garden carrying two buckets of water, and stopped when she saw Miranda.

Miranda was glad to have missed another confrontation. She drove off, happy that she had gone back, and happy that it was over. That's that, she told herself.

*

Miranda rubbed lotion on her hands and arms after her bath. Ben was downstairs working on a floor plan, as he often did at night. She heard a car door slam and went to look out the bedroom window. William had parked in the rear of the garden house. When he opened the back door, golden lamp light poured outside, and then disappeared when he shut the door.

Miranda read for a while in bed, reading the same page over and over. She eventually turned off the light and fell asleep. She woke up once when Ben came to bed, and then she fell into a restless sleep.

From somewhere, she heard a cry, and her sleeping mind wove the sound into her dream.

She was walking outside when she heard a voice calling out, a child's frightened voice. She wanted to find the boy and protect him. She followed his cries to an old abandoned outbuilding, gray and dilapidated; she entered.

Everything was old, dusty, jumbled. Odd flights of stairs led in different directions but didn't connect with each other, or dead-ended against the walls. She climbed up one flight of stairs, hearing the tiny voice. At the top, she came to a room full of doors and cupboards. She tried to open them.

"Where are you?" she called.

"I'm here," came his voice.

She followed his voice to a door, but it didn't have a handle. She ran her hands around the frame. "Who are you? Are you hurt?"

"Johnny. Don't tell him where I am."

She tried to press the door open. She heard footsteps behind her and quickly turned around.

Miranda woke, her heart still pounding. She sat up and listened. Again, she thought she heard a cry and cocked her head to listen. But all was silent. She nudged Ben and whispered, "Ben. Ben!"

He sleepily rolled over. "Hmm?"

"Ben, did you hear anything?"

That caught his attention. "In the house?"

"No. Outside. A cry or something. I had a dream. And it was so real. There was a child. Trapped behind a wall. I couldn't get to him, but some guy was going to hurt him."

"Just a dream."

"But I'm sure I heard a cry."

"Probably Paula's cat."

Miranda lay back down. Ben put his arm around her, and soon his breathing became deep and rhythmic. She pulled the cover up, and fell back asleep.

*

The next morning, Miranda was buttering some English muffins when Ben came into the kitchen.

"The coffee's ready," she said. "Do you want an egg, or oatmeal?"

"No. This is fine." Ben poured out a cup of coffee, added some milk, and took a few sips. Then he stopped, leaned back in his chair, and turned his head to Miranda.

"Am I starting to have weird dreams now, or did you wake me in the middle of the night to tell me about a trapped kid?"

It sounded ridiculous in the sunlight and solid shapes of morning. But Miranda still had a sense of something being wrong. "It was so real, Ben. You know how some dreams are like that? It was like I was there and could hear him. I've had several of these dreams now, about the same little boy." She hesitated a moment before continuing. "I'm beginning to think they mean something."

Ben looked up, doubtful. "Like what?"

"I don't know. What if there's a child trapped somewhere? That's the feeling I get. And that dream about the predator. And the daycare incident. It all makes sense. Somehow."

"Our man Jasper," said Ben, and bit into the English muffin. "Besides, you said nothing happened at the daycare."

Everything was starting to get mixed up. Dreams, rumors, her insecurities. "I know it sounds crazy – but haven't you ever had a flash of intuition, when you just know something?"

"No. I haven't. Look, Miranda. The kids are fine. You speak to them every day. It's that shelter. You said so yourself. I don't want you going back there."

She leaned against the counter, considering his words. "No, that's not it." She sat down and wrapped her hands around her coffee cup, as if for warmth. "Anyway, I told you, I'm not going back. I brought the last of the clothes."

"Good. Then the dreams will stop." Ben took another bite. "I think you just need to move on with things."

"What does that mean?" Miranda asked defensively.

"Just that – the kids are gone. And you need to find something else to fill your time."

"You think I'm fabricating dreams to fill my time?! My God, Ben, my sense of self is a little stronger than that."

"I'm not saying that, but you're letting these dreams get in your way. You spent so much of your time with the kids, and now that they're gone – "

"I don't believe it! You think I have empty nest syndrome. I hate that expression. It makes women sound like they have only one purpose in life. That's really outdated, Ben."

"I didn't say that. You did. I'm just saying now's your chance to do something else. For a change."

They ate in silence, Miranda wondering why she had snapped at Ben. Perhaps she was living in her head too much. She reached for the brochure from Paula, glanced at it, and handed it to him. "Paula told me about it."

Ben scanned it. "You going to go?"

"I might. Maybe I'll get some ideas." She sipped her coffee.

He nodded as he read the brochure. "This is a great idea. I've always told you that you should try to sell your work. And that's what you've always wanted. If you could treat it as a business, it might make it more tangible, more achievable."

Miranda knew that Ben saw her as too unfocused, jumping from project to project. And she knew that he was right. "That makes sense."

"I could help with that part of it, the business side," said Ben.

Miranda inwardly cringed at the word *business*, envisioning spreadsheets and ledgers, a pencil behind her ear.

Ben gave a quick nod, as if all was settled. "It's a great idea. I'm glad you're going."

"I said I was *thinking* about it."

Ben picked up his briefcase and the set of drawings, and kissed her goodbye. "See you tonight."

Miranda brought the dishes to the sink, casting a glance now and then at the brochure.

She leaned against the counter with a hand on her hip. Then she dumped her cold coffee into the sink, and poured herself a fresh cup. She sat at the table and began to read the brochure more closely. Perhaps if it was a business, she would work on schedule rather than waiting for the time to be right. Maybe there was something to that. It had certainly worked for Paula.

Miranda tried to imagine herself with the same excitement Paula had when she talked about profit margin and cash flow and marketing ideas, but no enthusiasm arose within her.

Rather, what excited her was a new idea for a piece, wet clay in her hands, squeezing out a glob of cobalt blue onto a palette, forming a pattern out of mosaics. She feared that at heart she was not marketable, and that the only thing her creative endeavors would ever produce was, as Paula might say, a negative cash flow.

And yet it was Paula's love of things that got her started with her business – her passion for finding and then transforming old, discarded, ordinary objects into something interesting or beautiful. She had turned her love for shopping at garage sales and flea markets into a thriving small business. Her first store in Wallingford had done so well that she had opened a larger one in Bellevue, and was planning a third store that her sister would run in the San Juan Islands. She had never seen Paula so happy and energetic. Why shouldn't she be able to do the same?

The ill-defined unease that had haunted her lately was gradually being replaced by the solidity of a practical plan. The seminar would be the first step. She would at least go and hear what they had to say.

She went to the calendar, circled the date, and wrote *Small Business Seminar*. Now she had something concrete to hold onto, to focus her energy on. She was tired of moping, tired of analyzing her dreams and imagining crazy things. What she needed was to get busy and start making things happen. Like Paula. Like Ben.

Miranda laced up her running shoes, and started on a brisk walk. She took the same route as she had the other day. When she reached the top of the hill, she looked over again at the house with the swimming pool, but she didn't see the champagne-drinking artist.

But ever since that day, Miranda had begun noticing other older women who inspired her. Whether she was at the health food store or nursery, at a restaurant or in one of the neighborhood shops, she noticed women who moved with purpose, and laughed with gusto, women who dressed with style, and who seemed to live with passion.

Miranda enjoyed the challenge of the steep hill, and soon worked up a sweat. She would go home, shower, and make a salad. Register for the seminar, and read the book from Paula. From this point on, her life would move forward, not backwards, or worse, remain in that awful stagnation where nothing happened.

When she reached her street again, she saw Nicole up ahead with her two kids. Though it had been Miranda's firm intention to stop thinking about trapped kids and predators and the daycare and the cries at night, the momentum of those thoughts had not yet come to a halt. She didn't want to give in to an overactive imagination – but it couldn't hurt to ask.

Nicole and her kids were peering inside a tall bush. Nicole noticed her coming, and waved.

"Hi, Miranda!"

"Good morning! Hi, Danny. Hello, Ariel," Miranda said, bending down to them. "What have you found?"

"Shhh!" said Danny, pointing into the bush.

Miranda peeked in and saw an empty bird's nest. She opened her eyes wide to the gratification of the little boy and girl. "Wow! A bird's nest."

"But the babies are gone," said Ariel.

Danny pointed up to the trees. "That's the mommy bird. She's teaching them how to fly."

Miranda lifted her eyes to the crows in a tall pine, and exchanged a smile with Nicole.

While Danny and Ariel poked around the bushes for another nest, Miranda spoke softly to Nicole. "I meant to ask you – Did something happen at the daycare? Paula mentioned something the other day."

It took Nicole a moment to realize what Miranda was referring to. "Oh, that," she laughed. "You know Dillon? Well, his mother started a new job, so his grandfather had to pick him up. Dillon wasn't ready to leave, so he put up quite a fight. Danny came home telling me that some man tried to kidnap Dillon. I knew the school would have notified me. Still, I called his teacher, just to make sure." Nicole put a hand on Miranda's arm. "Last week he had me believing there was a snake under his bed. He can be pretty convincing."

Miranda had to laugh at the antics of Danny. He was now on his hands and knees digging in the dirt with a stick. "I'm glad that's all it was." Miranda felt a sense of relief and realized she had been worrying about the incident. It had sat at the back of her mind, seeking out an explanation.

Nicole made a face of repugnance. "Danny! Put that down." He found a worm and was trying to put it in the nest. Nicole shook her head, and steered the kids ahead of her. "See you, Miranda!"

Miranda waved goodbye and watched them go. She remembered taking Michael and Clara on such walks of exploration at that age, and how they delighted in the discovery of a mushroom, a curl of madrona bark, a snail clinging to the underside of a stem, and Michael's favorite, the glistening trails of the slugs.

After one such walk, she had made a little painting for Michael. A background of textured shades of green and brown, suggestive of moss, grass, leaves. And then running diagonally, a meandering, looping line of silver paint, with just the tip of a slug exiting the canvas corner.

She hadn't expected him to love it so much, but it had hung in his bedroom for years, and went with him for three semesters in a dorm room. It was now in his Portland apartment. It touched her that it still mattered to him. The same way Clara had taken a small fairy painting with her to San Francisco, and one of the rosebud topiaries they had made together.

Though she fought against the impulse, Miranda called Clara when she got home – but she was at the gym and couldn't really talk. Then she spoke to Michael for a minute before he left to have lunch with a co-worker. She briefly told them both about the seminar, and that Paula had sold some of her pieces, and that she had just gotten back from a walk and was getting into shape.

The truth was she still had to have some daily contact with them, even if it was just an email or text message, or the day just didn't feel right. It would be like going a whole day without speaking to Ben.

After her shower she felt refreshed, full of energy. She browsed through her clothes, considering what to wear to the seminar, and pulled out a couple of items that she thought were appropriate for business. They were bland and boring, but practical – clothes she had bought during the few years she had done office work, after Ben switched jobs. She had held onto them just in case she ever needed to go back to work.

Standing in front of the mirror, she tried on a few possibilities, and grew increasingly frustrated with each piece. Her old skirts and pants were too tight; she would definitely have to try a different dry cleaner. She hadn't gained that much weight. Had she? She wished Clara were there, to get an honest opinion. Ben always said everything looked great.

She held up a few jackets and blouses, frowned, and decided on a black pantsuit and one of two shirts.

As she returned the clothes to the back of her closet, she saw the old pieces she hadn't been able to part with – clothing from when she dressed in a way that wasn't determined by office dress code, and before she started wearing comfortable mom clothes. There they were – her long skirts, some embroidered, some beaded. She pulled out a deep midnight blue skirt that shimmered with movement, and a vintage print blouse. Just the glimpse of them filled her with a deep yearning for her younger days. She returned them, closed the closet door, and went downstairs.

But a trace of that old excitement stubbornly stayed with her. There's no reason why I can't recreate that earlier feeling, she thought. It could be even better. I have the man I love, I have a family. I don't have the anxiety over money that I used to have, or the pressure of which path to pursue.

Or did those worries and concerns help to fuel that earlier drive, making everything more intense, more urgent, more exciting? Perhaps. But she was a different woman now. Her approach to life was different.

And yet it's not too late, she told herself. Look at Paula. Look at the woman by the pool. Many women come into their own later in life.

Miranda curled up with a cup of tea and Paula's book on how to attract the life you want. For the most part, she was familiar with the sometimes trite, neatly packaged ideas. Still, she thought, it doesn't stop them from being true.

Her skepticism diminished as she read on, and she became more excited, realizing how she was preventing herself from having the kind of life she wanted. She was amazed to find that even her thinking had changed over the years. She used to approach life with such openness and energy, believing in her dreams.

For so long her life had been consumed with the kids and Ben – the vacations, the holidays, the homework and sports and camps, the parties and sleepovers. She had loved it all. Every minute of it.

But now, for the first time, she realized that she needed to reclaim, to awaken from slumber, the part of herself that used to steer her life. Perhaps this seminar really could be the beginning of something. This could be a time to blossom, to bloom into full being.

She jumped up when she heard Ben come home.

"You're home early?" she asked.

"No – I'm late, actually."

Miranda glanced at the clock. "I didn't know it was so late. I was just reading that book Paula gave me and getting some ideas."

"You look all fired up," Ben said.

"I am. I feel awake. You're right. It's time for me to make some changes, start making things again."

Ben smiled. "*These* are the kinds of dreams I like you to have."

She was about to object to his remark, but his warm smile told her that he was sincerely happy for her.

Chapter 7

~

Miranda drove home from the seminar filled with a sense of defeat. From the beginning, everything had gone wrong. She had arrived late because she couldn't find parking and had to park ten blocks away. Then it began to drizzle, and unable to find her umbrella in the car, she had shown up damp and disheveled, and flustered from her rush. Then just as she made her way to a seat, bumping knees and apologizing, her phone rang, earning her a sarcastic reminder from the lecturer about house rules.

Nevertheless, once the seminar got underway, Miranda enthusiastically jotted down notes on strategy, goals, and objectives. But when the subject shifted to market analysis and competitive analysis, operations and management, her eyes began to glaze over. At one point, she realized that she was sketching flowers in the border of her notebook. She crossed them out and tried to focus.

After lunch, they formed breakout groups and began hammering out their business plans. Miranda was thrown when they went around the table and introduced their product or service. Unprepared, she said, "I make things. I recently sold a mosaic planter." The group smiled politely.

From that point, she felt outside the discussion, a spectator watching the other participants. Everyone was several stages ahead of her, clear about their goals, brisk in their calculations. Feeling both overwhelmed and discouraged, Miranda left the seminar early, her feet hurting, and more confused than ever about what direction to take. At the root of everything was frustration with herself, that she hadn't planned her life better.

When she arrived home, she caught a glimpse of herself in the hall mirror. The drab black suit and burgundy blouse looked awful on her, harsh and stiff. And it didn't help that the speaker had worn the same colors.

Miranda kicked off the shoes that pinched her feet, promising herself that was the last time she would ever wear anything so uncomfortable. How – and why – had she ever worn such shoes? They were almost as high as the stilettos the speaker wore, clacking about the stage.

The suit was going to the Salvation Army, she decided, tossing it on her bedroom floor. Along with the shoes. She wondered why she had so quickly abandoned her resolution to be herself, to dress how she wanted, say what she wanted. Instead, she had sat through the draining seminar uncomfortable and silent.

She pulled on her jeans and an old sweatshirt, took off her "office" earrings and set them on her dresser. She opened her jewelry box and looked at her vintage pieces. Then she lifted out a long strand of gray and gold crystal beads that she bought long ago. I should have worn them, she thought. And a spangled skirt. That's what the woman by the pool would have done. She slipped the necklace over her head.

While she boiled water for tea, Miranda called Clara. Then Michael. Voicemail for both. Just as well, she thought. What news did she have anyway? She left a message for Ben saying the seminar was not what she expected and that she had left early and was now at home.

She looked out the kitchen window. The morning rain was long gone; sunshine filled the garden with a gentle, dappled light. All she wanted was to sit in her garden. She would take her tea out there, and do nothing.

Her habit, when she felt far from herself, was to latch on to the things she loved: comfortable clothes, her pretty things, her garden. She reached for her favorite teacup – an antique with pink roses, green leaves, and dots of gold paint along the rim – and took out a tin of loose, black tea. She poured the water over the tea and let it steep until it was strong and dark, and then added honey and cream. Any idea of dieting and working out could just wait.

Miranda took her tea out to the garden. The ground was still damp beneath her bare feet, but the bench with the little table next to it was dry. She curled up on it, and took a sip of the rich, fragrant tea. That first hot, sweet sip was always heaven. A sigh released from deep inside. Home. She was home and everything would be all right.

She cradled the teacup in her hands. Preparing her tea with honey and cream always reminded her of the early days on her own, when she had moved to the University District and found the upstairs of an old house to rent. It had a small deck surrounded by tall bushes that bloomed over the railing – long arcs of purple butterfly flowers, white snowball bushes, melon-colored quince in the spring. She used to snip off the blooms and put them in vases in her kitchen and bedroom – sometimes even in the bathroom. That still seemed like the ultimate indulgence – fresh flowers in the bathroom. Ironic, she thought. Now that she had a garden, she rarely did that. Only when guests came.

What had changed in her? When had she stopped living in that poor, but extravagant manner?

Or had it simply been the excitement of having her own apartment that inspired her to live so richly? Though she never had enough money to properly furnish the space, and it remained largely empty, she had loved that old house. She sketched and painted the flowers she picked, and hung the drawings on the wall, so that even in winter she was surrounded with color and blooms.

Little by little, she had added to her place. At a neighborhood thrift store, she found a charming wooden table and chairs set, and a dresser that she painted in a color she always thought of as *seaside cottage green*. From an odds and ends shop, she bought an old wrought iron mirror encircled with ivy; she then set a vase of peacock feathers in front of it, doubling the iridescent blues and greens.

One day, in front of one of the beautiful old homes in the neighborhood, she saw a pile of furniture with a sign that read *Free/Salvation Army*. She carried home the black iron head-and-footboards and made another trip to get the bedrails. Then she spray-painted the bed gold and thought that it was beautiful.

For the living room, she bought a Victorian floral rug that covered most of the floor. There was a worn spot in the middle, but she covered it with a small table draped in an old lace tablecloth – and was amazed at the transformation of the room when she set a vase of flowers on the table, and turned on the lamp.

Those were lean days, going to school, working at various jobs – waitressing, the department store, office temping. But those were the days when she had discovered the little indulgences that made her feel rich, indulgences that she had taken with her through life: a pot of strong black tea, fresh flowers, long walks, hot baths. She remembered the walks through the neighborhood she used to take, over Ravenna bridge and down through the park. That beautiful park with paths crossing down to the bottom. Sometimes she would go there barefoot, in a simple sundress, and imagine that it was some sort of magical land.

Probably not a good idea, she now thought. I could have gotten tetanus. But back then she was free-spirited, naïve, and romantic. With a shudder, she remembered how one afternoon, she caught a small movement out of the corner of her eye. She glanced up the hill, and saw that a man had been watching her, from behind a tree. On being discovered, he slowly slid back behind the tree trunk. The magic of the park had vanished that day, and she never went back there alone.

She remembered carrying her laundry several blocks away, up and down the steep, slatted sidewalk. Miranda sipped the last of her tea and thought how hard it was back then. And yet she had found time to read and draw, to dance in the living room, to dream. What happened to that old self, to that open, wondrous way of living?

She looked down at the dregs in her cup. Age had happened. Responsibilities. Creepy men in the park. The few friends she had back then, artists mostly, had moved away, or she had lost touch with them. When the landlord sold the house, she moved into an apartment, and got rid of the beautiful old rug that she could never get the dust out of. Somewhere along the way, she had learned that the dust motes she romanticized about when the afternoon shafts of light poured through the living room windows, were actually dust mites – another illusion dashed. One by one, the dream bubbles of youth had vanished – either popping on their own, or floating away beyond sight.

Now, here she was, fifty. The struggle and day-to-day difficulties of life were gone. She was grateful for the laundry room in the house, for her garden, for the comforts and beauty of her home. She had Ben to thank for that. Though money had always been an issue, they had managed. There had been some difficult periods, but they had gotten through them, and were able to give the kids a happy childhood.

She looked out at her garden and could almost see the kids hunting for frogs and chasing butterflies, Clara helping her find sticks for her rosebud topiaries, Michael and his friends digging in the soil, picnics spread on blankets.

So far away now, the kids. She missed their rambunctious ways, missed the gratification of fulfilling even their tiniest needs, missed listening to their stories and adventures, and encouraging their dreams.

All gone now – her youth, their childhood. She swallowed and her vision blurred, and when she tried to set her teacup on the table, she missed the edge and it fell, shattering on the flagstone. With a gasp she knelt down beside it, seeing the pink and green and gold shards as a symbol of her life.

"Good afternoon!"

Miranda jumped up, unreasonably startled by William.

"Sorry," he said. "I didn't mean to – I seem to have a way of coming upon you by surprise."

Miranda couldn't help thinking, well if you would make a little more noise. "Hi, William. I thought you were gone." She turned away and used the neck of her sweatshirt to dab at her eyes.

"No, I was just writing down below and thought I'd cut through the garden and walk to the park." He hesitated a moment. "Is everything okay?"

Miranda tried to laugh away whatever impression she had made. "Yes – just – thinking of stuff." She didn't want to talk about youthful dreams and missing the kids. "I went to a seminar and it didn't go very well. I mean – it wasn't what I thought it would be."

"Well, maybe there's one that would suit you better. What was it about?" he asked tentatively.

Miranda sat back on the bench and motioned for him to have a seat. She really just wanted to be alone with her thoughts, but William had such a gentle way about him, and so rarely initiated a conversation, that she wanted to welcome him.

"I won't bore you with the details. I've been thinking about – I'm trying to figure out what it is I want to do with my life, you know, now that I have a little more time," she said, planning to leave it at that.

"Do you have any ideas? What sort of things do you like?"

"Well, part of the problem is that I really don't have anything – any skill – that's marketable. I've always been a bit of a dabbler. I didn't finish college..." She let her words trail off, feeling that she was underrating herself, yet also feeling that it was the truth.

"What did you study?"

"Art. Art history. I thought I wanted to be a teacher. But..."

"Would you like to go back to school?"

She leaned her head to the side, and considered once again the option she had always decided against. "I don't think so. Not now. I guess I should have earlier. Though to tell the truth, I was always a bit at odds with it."

William smiled. "School isn't always the answer. The secret is to find what gives you the most satisfaction, the most meaning. Don't you think?"

"Yes, I do. I think that's why this business seminar just didn't click." She looked out at the garden, as if pondering something. "I've been a mom for so long. That's how I see myself. I keep drawing a blank when I try to remember what I was going to do with my life. I used to want – so many things. But I didn't really follow through with any of them."

"Maybe you just need to find a way to reconnect with your earlier dreams."

Miranda turned to William, surprised that he understood. "That's exactly what I've been thinking."

She looked back out at the garden. "The thing is, I liked being a mom. That's something I was good at," she said, her voice quivering.

"There's no reason you can't be a mom and still do other things." He lifted a leaf from a nearby bush and examined the front, the back. "Someone wrote that mothers are the caretakers of the world."

Miranda laughed. "You don't have to glorify it for my sake." She gave him a sidelong glance. "Isn't that a rather old-fashioned idea for a young college professor to have?"

"I don't mean that women should be confined to the home – far from it. What I mean to say is…" He looked away.

"What?"

He shook his head, as if it was just an idle thought not worth saying. "Just something I was thinking while I was sitting down there in the garden."

"Tell me. I'd like to know."

He gazed down towards the lower garden, as if gathering up his thoughts from there. "Well, I was sitting – actually, lying there – in the hammock. It was so peaceful. The wind chimes ringing, the mild breeze. And I was thinking that in all my studies and teaching and research, in all the books I've read, there's nothing that quite compares to the idea of home." He turned to Miranda when he said the word *home*, as if referring to an abstract concept, rather than to something immediate and familiar, as it was for her. "I mean, it's so simple and something we take for granted but…" Again, he let his words trail off.

Miranda faced him, intrigued by what he was getting at. "Go on."

"What I mean to say is – there are a lot of beautiful ideas out there, but, at its best, the idea of *home* is hard to top." He lifted his eyes to the garden and the house. "When it's a place of refuge, a place of love and meaning where memories are born and nourished. When it becomes a part of you that you carry through life." He became suddenly self-conscious and waved away the idea.

Miranda looked down. Those were her feelings too, about home, the garden, family – though she had never thought about them in that exact way. They sat quietly for a few moments.

William reached down and picked up a tiny pinecone from the ground and began turning it around in his fingers, examining it intently. "Last night, I was out walking. It was dark and drizzling. And I passed your house on my way back. The light was on. I heard laughter and the smells of cooking, and I thought: 'How beautiful! How simple, and how beautiful.' To be raised in such a way must make a person secure and hopeful, to be rooted in a place so full of meaning." He stopped speaking and shrugged, and tossed the pinecone back down.

Miranda thought about his words and looked out at the garden. "You know, as a mom, you spend a good chunk of your life raising your kids. You get so involved with their lives. Then, poof! All of a sudden, they're gone. But if I've helped to create a place of home inside of them, as you say, that they'll always have – well, that's enough."

With a smile, Miranda remembered the home of her youth. "I guess I had that to a large extent growing up. We didn't have much money, but there was always good food, music, laughter. I feel sorry for anybody who didn't have that."

"Yes," William said. "To miss out on and never know something so fundamental."

Miranda sat up and faced William, ready to fight against such an idea. "Oh, I hope not! Surely it's never too late to create that place for yourself – at any age. Surely it's never too late to surround yourself with the things you love, the people you love. To make new memories. Isn't that a lifelong process?"

William considered the idea. "I'm not so sure –"

They were interrupted by the sound of a car pulling in the driveway, and saw that Ben was home.

William rose to his feet. "Sorry. I didn't mean to get all philosophical."

Miranda also stood. "No, I'm glad for our conversation. You've made me see things from a different angle. You kind of validated everything I've been feeling." She waved over at Ben. "Why don't you come up to the house – join us out on the deck?"

William picked up his notebook. "Thanks, but I need to run a few errands. I didn't realize it was so late." He raised his head in greeting to Ben, and then went back down through the garden.

"Feel free to stop by anytime, William!" she called out, hoping he didn't think that now Ben was home, she was no longer interested in talking with him.

She walked up to the house and met Ben just as he was coming out of the garage.

He gave her a quick kiss and lifted the antique strand of beads. "Interesting look," he said, causing Miranda to laugh. "So the seminar wasn't what you thought it would be?"

"No, it wasn't. Though I have to say, it matters less after my conversation with William." She looked back at the garden, seeing everything differently. She had lost sight of some of her earlier dreams, but the essence was still there, an integral part of her life.

"It looked like you were deep in conversation. What were you talking about?"

"Nothing in particular. But he really lifted my spirits. He's such a nice guy." She linked her arm with Ben's. "Come. I'll get dinner ready and tell you all about it."

They sat out on the deck and over dinner Miranda related some of the advice William had given her. Then she described the disastrous morning, how it had started with arriving late, the rain, and then her phone ringing.

"Sorry," Ben said. "I thought you said it started at 10:30."

"I thought it did. I must have read it wrong."

"Well, there will be other seminars."

"I know. That's what William said."

Ben couldn't help feeling slightly put off. It seemed that William had a sudden, and unearned, influence over Miranda.

"Maybe I should have stayed. I don't know why I gave up so easily."

"Sometimes that's your solution."

"You don't have to remind me of my failures, Ben."

"I'm not doing that. I'm just saying that sometimes you have to push through things." After a moment, he rubbed her arm. "Anyway, give yourself credit for going. Did you get anything out of it? Any information?"

Miranda didn't want to talk about it anymore, but she knew this was Ben's way of apologizing. "Maybe a little. The importance of tracking expenses, measuring results, that kind of thing."

Ben nodded encouragingly. "That's good. It's a start."

Then she told him about the breakout groups and how it had all felt over her head. "I just gave up, doubting whether a business would be the right thing."

"You could start small and see how it goes. I can help you set it up."

She put her hand on his arm. "Thanks. I'll think about it."

"I really think it would be good for you," Ben said. "A way to get out from under the influence of those dreams you've been having. It's like they're preventing you from moving forward."

Miranda opened her mouth to dispute the idea, but changed her mind, not wanting to argue. Besides, even though Ben didn't understand the power of an intuition, she knew there was some truth to his words. The dreams were preoccupying her more than she cared to admit. She nodded as if in agreement. She then leaned over to the trellis, picked a sprig of climbing jasmine, and held the sweetness to her nose.

"You know," said Miranda, "I was so upset when I came home. I was mad at the speaker, mad at myself, at a loss." She shook her head at each remembrance. "Then I came home and sat out in the garden."

"Your refuge."

She smiled and nodded. "I got all sad about my old dreams never amounting to anything, just feeling bad. Then William came up and we talked a bit. And somehow I saw the bigger picture. And I felt good about who I am."

"Don't I make you feel like that?" Ben asked with an easy laugh, but there was a hint of hurt in his eyes.

"Yes," Miranda said qualitatively.

"But?"

Miranda lifted her shoulders. "I guess I needed to hear it from someone else. William really knows how to listen."

"And I don't? You see? You always value someone else's opinion over mine. I tell you that all the time."

"What are you getting so testy about?" Miranda started to clear off the table. "You need to start getting some exercise, Ben."

"Me? You're the one who thinks the dry cleaner is shrinking all your clothes." He stood and lifted his plate.

Miranda started to take the plate from his hand. "Never mind. I'll clean up."

"I'll get it." Ben held onto the plate, stacked a few dishes on top of it, and brought them inside.

They both loaded the dishwasher, banging the dishes and growing more annoyed as they got in each other's way.

Miranda was beginning to feel like a yoyo – getting excited, then depressed, then feeling good, then bad. "I'm going upstairs."

Ben reached out to her, but she turned and left before she noticed his gesture. He finished up in the kitchen, hearing the water run upstairs. He rested one hand on the counter, and stared down at the floor.

Then he took a cigar and a lighter and went back out onto the deck. He sank into a chair and lit his cigar. From down below, he saw William arrive back home, park the car, and enter the garden house.

Ben leaned back in his chair, resting his eyes on the window upstairs where Miranda was taking her bath. Then he looked down at the lighted window in the garden house, and ever so slightly narrowed his eyes in thought.

*

That night Miranda dreamed again about the trapped child and the strange building.

Again, she followed the sounds of pleading voices and scuffling. She hurried up a flight of stairs, and from one landing she saw across to a room off another stairway.

This time there were two children, a boy and a girl. A man grabbed the girl's hair and pulled her roughly to him. The boy kicked him repeatedly, until the man pushed him down and placed a heavy foot on his back. The boy squeezed his eyes shut in pain.

Miranda ran down the stairs and across the room, searching for a way to get to the children. But there was no staircase leading to them.

Miranda awoke, raised her head, and listened. Then she jostled Ben. "Ben!"

He grunted but kept his back to her.

"Ben, I had another dream. I really think there's a child in danger."

He groaned. "Not this again."

"The dreams are so real. I know they mean something. I can feel it." She waited for him to say something, and then gave him a light nudge.

"Why don't you discuss it with William?" he said.

Miranda sat up, furious at his comment. Then she rolled onto her side and punched up her pillow, wondering why she had bothered trying to talk to Ben about it.

Chapter 8

~

Miranda woke up late, feeling groggy and irritable. She heard Ben in the kitchen, and hurried downstairs only to see him grab an apple and his briefcase before heading out the door.

"Aren't you going to eat anything?" she asked.

"I'm late as it is."

She followed him to the door. "Don't forget – Paula and Derek are coming to dinner tonight."

He made no comment, but walked to his car and got inside.

Miranda waited to see if he would turn around and wave, but he gave no sign that he noticed her. She went back inside and closed the door, thinking what a stubborn man he was.

After getting dressed and having a bite to eat, she went to the garage and brought the bag of old china to the bench outside the front door. She was determined to complete one of her projects – in part to prove to Ben, and herself, that she could. She looked at the stack of cracked and chipped china from one of her visits to a flea market with Paula. Several years ago. Her intention had been to make a mosaic mirror, but she had never gotten around to it.

Today was the day she would follow through with it. Tomorrow she would begin on the screen. No more excuses.

She spread newspapers in front of the bench, and set the stack of plates on them, along with a small hammer. As she examined the dishes, she tried not to think about the recurring dreams, or about Ben's dismissive attitude towards them. Of course, most of the times her dreams didn't mean anything at all. But there had been times when they did. She supposed they came from minute perceptions that her subconscious mind picked up on, and when they reached a tipping point, she had a dream, telling her to pay attention.

But this time, she didn't know what to pay attention to. There were only three things different in her life: the kids both moving away at the same time, the visits to the shelter, and the arrival of William. The kids were fine; in her heart, she knew the dreams were not about them. And though she had been initially upset about the shelter, it hadn't left any deep impression. And

William – she turned her head towards the garden house, considering if there could be anything concerning him. He was a nice guy, quiet and gentle. He had made her feel better about herself yesterday.

She leaned back against the bench, realizing that she wasn't being entirely honest with herself. There was another feeling about William she was ignoring, one she didn't want to examine. There was something mysterious about him, secretive. She was almost one hundred percent sure that the cries she heard at night were coming from the garden house. Had he brought someone there? Why did she always get the feeling that he was hiding something? She shook away the thought, feeling ungenerous in her suspicions.

She put on a pair of gardening gloves and lifted the hammer. It was Ben she was upset with. He could be so infuriating, she thought, lifting the first plate and giving it a light tap – then a series of stronger taps, until it shattered. She always listened to and supported him. Why wasn't he doing the same for her? She smashed another plate, and then a saucer. Making her feel like she had nothing better to do than conjure up some drama because her life was temporarily empty. She smashed several more plates, then set the hammer down, and studied the mess. Was he right? Here I am, fifty, and completely unsure of myself, my perceptions, my feelings.

After smashing the last dish, she stood stiffly, and looked down at the shattered china – and felt overwhelmed that she was supposed to make sense of the fragments, give them some shape of beauty. She pulled off the gardening gloves, and dropped them onto the newspapers. She would do the shopping for tonight's dinner; get that out of the way. Continue with the mosaic project in the afternoon.

Miranda first stopped off at the nursery to pick up some rose food. As usual, she spent more time than she intended, wandering the aisles, stopping to decide between several colors of dianthus. Across the shades of pink, purple, and red flowers, she saw a young teen who reminded her of the girl at the shelter. Miranda remembered the girl digging in the hard soil with the old, bent spoon. Why hadn't she done more to help the girl?

She went back to the store entrance, took a flat cart, and began to load it with potting soil, a few simple gardening tools, and several flats of flowers for both sun and shade. She stood in front of the gardening gloves and started to lift down a cloth pair. Then she put them back, and reached for the supple leather ones, remembering the thrill of slipping on a new pair. A bubble of happiness arose in her at the thought of introducing that thrill to someone else – though the girl might just as well hurl them back and call her more names.

Miranda drove back to the shelter. The girl was working in the little garden along with another girl, so engrossed in weeding that she didn't notice Miranda going up the steps. Miranda went inside and spoke to the woman behind the desk. Soon, three teens were helping to carry the gardening items from her car to the garden.

The girl stood up, shading her eyes from the sun, astonished at the supplies and flowers being placed at her feet.

"I brought some things for the garden," Miranda said simply. The girl could do with them what she wanted.

The girl looked down at all the items, then up at Miranda. "Why?" she asked, without a trace of sarcasm.

"Here," said Miranda, ignoring her question. She lifted the tools from the bag and handed them to the girl. "These will make it easier to dig." She pointed to the potting soil. "Mix some of this into the soil around the plants. And this will help." She pulled out a canister of plant food. "Good luck."

Miranda started to leave, but the girl called out to her. "Wait!"

Miranda turned, not sure what to expect.

The girl averted her eyes, struggling with what to say. "I'm sorry about the other day. When – " she looked back to the garden, "when you said that about bleeding hearts, I thought you were taking a jab at me. I thought you were saying that I couldn't take it." Her expression changed to one of sweetness and vulnerability, revealing another side of her. "I didn't know there really was such a flower as a bleeding heart. Until it bloomed. Look!" She walked to the shady area of the garden beneath the tree and bent down to the little bush. Then she gently lifted a thin branch with delicate pink and white hearts dangling from it.

Miranda kneeled and cradled the tiny flowers in her hand. "They're one of my favorites. They'll only bloom for a month or so. I have some of these in my garden, and a few in red and white." She stood, and extended her hand. "I'm Miranda."

The girl timidly placed her hand in Miranda's. "I'm Zoe." She shyly pointed to the girl reading in a chair, and another girl sitting on the grass near the garden. "They like it out here – now that there's something to look at. I found the chair a couple of blocks over, set out with the garbage. I brought it back and painted it. One of the guys helped me. It's like we have a space that's just for us, you know." She pointed to the girl sitting on the grass. "She always asks if she can do the watering."

"I guess everyone likes something to care for. Especially a garden." Miranda gazed down at the sparse plants scattered about the garden. "You'll be getting some blooms soon."

Zoe watched Miranda as she spoke, and then looked down at all the garden supplies. "Why – why did you do this?" she asked.

Miranda lifted her shoulders and smiled. "Just one gardener to another. You're off to a good start – and having the right tools is important. Oh," she said, remembering. She reached down into the bag and lifted out the leather gardening gloves. "You'll need these."

Zoe took the leather gloves and handled them as if they were velvet. "I'm supposed to dig with these?"

Miranda had to laugh. "I'm the same way. I always hate to get a new pair dirty. But the more you use them, the softer they get."

"Thank you," Zoe said, slipping on the gloves.

"Good luck with your garden, Zoe." Miranda gave a final glance at the garden, and began to leave.

Zoe followed Miranda a few steps and called to her. "Maybe you can come back sometime – to see how the garden turns out."

Miranda turned around and smiled at the invitation. "I'll be sure to do that."

Two more teens had gathered round the supplies. "Need some help, Zo?"

Miranda looked back and saw that Zoe was carefully examining the front and back of the gloves. She then reached down for the bag of potting soil and stood it on end. "We need to mix this into the soil first. Then we can plant the flowers."

*

Miranda stopped by the grocery store to pick up some last minute items for the dinner party. The usual excitement of preparing for such a gathering was dampened by the argument with Ben – though she wasn't even sure what they had argued about. She put the bags of groceries in the car and started to drive home.

Once again, she thought how short-lived her plans were to start a fresh chapter in her life. Ben was right – the nightmares she was having were clouding her vision and preventing her from moving forward. The little boy somehow locked her into the present, as if there were something she needed to do. She felt that he was calling out to her. How could she ignore that? And yet, if she wanted to move on, she would have to.

Then perhaps by trying not to think of the dreams, new and old dream images percolated up, haunting her, making her feel both angry and helpless. Images of the boy being flung down as he tried to defend himself. The boy with his shirt off, a ladder of red welts on his back. The doors with no handles. Johnny. She was sure it was the same boy in all the dreams. The car behind Miranda honked, making her jump, and she realized that the light had turned green. When the car honked again, she quickly turned at the corner to get out of its way.

After driving a few blocks, she found herself approaching the public pool. She flashed on the creepy man in the swimming pool dream. She slowed down and glanced over at the pool. Don't even *think* about it, she told herself. Just keep driving. You're not cut out for sleuthing. Besides, you don't even know what you're sleuthing about. Just a feeling.

Then she cast a look in her rear-view mirror and impulsively made a U-turn. She drove into the pool parking lot and turned off the car.

Why am I doing this? she wondered, surprised that she was so blindly following nothing more than a murky impulse. She knew the pool didn't have anything to do with the boy. If anything, she thought, I should be searching for a dilapidated building. Do I miss the kids more than I realize? Am I unconsciously trying to fill my life with purpose? Am I creating senseless drama?

She could imagine Ben sitting there next to her, the expression on his face telling her: This is going way too far. And her, stubbornly responding: It can't hurt to look. Then I can move on.

Miranda reached for her sunglasses and got out of the car. She walked to the chain-link fence surrounding the pool area and saw exactly what she expected to see: a swimming pool full of children playing, bobbing up and down in the water, holding their noses as they jumped off the sides. A few parents looked on, or chatted with each other. Some read books, others were in the water with their kids.

See it through, she told herself. Get it out of your system, once and for all. She walked up to the concession stand where two dripping kids were getting rainbow snow cones. She waited for the attendant to finish with them.

Was midlife crisis making her neurotic? Eccentric even? Would she soon be sipping champagne in the morning, dressed in flowing robes as she smashed more china?

Miranda watched the slow-moving teen hand out locker keys and towels. When he didn't seem to notice her, she stepped up and smiled. "Excuse me, I'm supposed to pick someone up. Would you mind paging them for me?"

The teen looked up. "The name?"

Miranda glanced around her, and leaned in. "Jasper," she said softly.

"Jasper what?"

Miranda shrank on hearing the name spoken aloud.

"Last name?" he pressed.

"Gosh, I can't remember. It's my cousin's friend, who's visiting."

"I need a last name." The teen waited, and then widened his eyes in impatience.

Miranda tapped her head. "Is it Wilson? Or Warren? Well, it's an unusual name. Just use the first name."

The teen shrugged and went to the intercom.

Miranda walked back to the fence where she could clearly see the pool area. Over the loudspeaker she heard: "Jasper, paging Jasper. Will Jasper please come to the concession stand? Your ride is here."

Miranda's heart beat faster on hearing the name being called out so loudly. She was suddenly afraid of what she was doing. What if she was dealing with someone dangerous? Why hadn't she thought of that? She closely examined the pool area, relieved that no one was taking any notice.

"Ma'am?" the teen at the counter called out, waiting to see if he was to try again.

Miranda shook her head and walked up to the counter. "He must have left already. Thank you."

She felt lighter as she headed back to her car. That's it, she told herself. I got it out of my system. Now I can go home and make moussaka, like a normal person. She opened her car door, and looked back at the pool, wondering how she could have been so foolish. Then she froze – there was William, standing outside the fence on the other side of the concession stand. He had on sunglasses and was watching the people at the pool. Something about it didn't feel right. She stared at him, wondering what he was doing.

He must have felt eyes on him, for he turned and looked directly at her.

Miranda stiffened, as if she had been caught at something, and then smiled. Then she realized that William had reacted in the same exact manner. He also appeared guilty, then quickly smiled and walked towards her.

She met him halfway. "William! What are you doing here?"

"Hi, Miranda. I heard there was a public pool nearby and thought I'd check it out. But I'd say it's a little too crowded for swimming laps. What about you?"

"Oh, I was looking for someone. I thought she might be here. But she's not."

Miranda stood uneasily for a moment, sensing that William knew she was lying, and suspecting that he was also lying. It felt especially awkward after their intimate conversation in the garden just yesterday. They seemed like different people today.

"So how are things?" Her voice sounded too cheerful, the tone all wrong, as if she hadn't seen him in ages.

"Fine, fine." William smiled and rubbed his foot against the pavement.

Miranda gestured behind her. "Well, I have groceries in the car – ice cream. Better go." She walked to her car and turned to wave goodbye. William was still standing where she had left him.

She drove off wondering how so much could change in a day. She was feeling more and more unsure of herself, of her judgment, of what everything meant. Her mind was a jumble – the dreams, the shelter, the argument with Ben, the kids, the conversation with William. Nothing added up. But foremost in her mind was a subtle shift towards William. She couldn't help seeing him in a different light. Why was he lying? What was he up to?

*

Miranda was behind schedule, busily preparing a salad for the dinner party, when she heard Ben pull in the driveway. She groaned as she remembered the mess of shattered china outside. She had completely forgotten about it.

Ben walked into the kitchen with a bunch of red roses, an expression of concern filling his face. "Hi, Honey – everything okay?"

"Everything's fine," she said, annoyed at his worried tone. She knew exactly what he was thinking – my wife is losing it, and now she's smashing dinner plates in front of the house before our guests arrive.

She lifted her cheek as he bent to kiss her. "I started on a project and then got interrupted." She noticed the stiff, store-bought roses in his hands, and turned back to the salad.

Ben glanced at the flowers and set them down on the counter. "I forgot. You don't like this kind."

She chopped the cucumbers with more vigor. "It's just that I've already picked flowers from the garden."

Ben looked over at the vases of fresh flowers in the dining room. "Seems like I can't get anything right lately."

"Oh, Ben, all I meant was…" She shook away her explanation. "They're very pretty. Thank you." She wondered why she was being so short with him. They rarely argued, but lately everything seemed to be spiraling downward.

She handed Ben a bowl of tabouli. "Can you set this on the table?" She smiled at him but he avoided her eyes and carried the bowl to the dining room. She filled a vase with water, trimmed the roses, and placed them in the vase. Just then the doorbell rang.

Ben answered the door, and showed Paula and Derek into the kitchen.

"Looks like someone had a meltdown outside," Derek laughed, setting a bottle of wine next to the red roses. "Nice flowers."

Paula put her face in the roses and inhaled. "No smell. But they're pretty."

Miranda saw the look on Ben's face and felt bad for him. "Aren't they? Ben brought them," she said, trying to sound as if she loved the flowers.

Derek sniffed the air. "Something sure smells good!"

Paula handed a small box to Miranda. "Baklava, in keeping with the Greek theme."

"Wonderful!" Miranda opened the box to show Ben, but he had already left the kitchen, saying he and Derek would be out on the deck.

Paula raised her eyebrows at Miranda.

Miranda ground pepper over the salad of tomatoes, cucumbers, red onion, and feta. "Just a little tension."

Paula bent over a dish of dolmades and olives. "Just one," she said, tasting an olive. "You haven't been yourself lately, Miranda. Like you're preoccupied or something."

"I've been thinking the same thing," she laughed. "I'm not sure what's going on with me." She went to the refrigerator and took out a platter of three different kinds of Greek dips. She then turned on the stove, added a touch of butter, and began to pan fry the pita bread.

"That looks delicious. Anything I can do?"

"How about opening the bottle of wine in the fridge? We'll start with white." She reached into the cupboard and lifted down the glasses.

"A brilliant idea," said Paula, reaching for the bottle of wine. "This will help to soften the edges." She opened the bottle and poured out two glasses.

Miranda flipped the pita bread, and then clinked her glass to Paula's. "To mid-life crisis."

Paula lifted her glass. "Hear, hear!"

*

Candle flames glinted off the glasses of red wine, and illuminated the small vases of multi-colored zinnias that were set among a spread of dips, bread, and salad. A dish of fragrant moussaka sat in the center of the table. Ben's mood improved as the evening wore on, as Miranda knew it would, with the effects of good food and good company – though Miranda thought he had drunk a little too much wine, which was unusual for him. He would have a headache tomorrow.

The four friends were enjoying one of their lively debates. Twice, Miranda had started to clear some of the dishes, but got caught up in the discussion and sat back down. Paula had asked Miranda if she was sleeping better, and the conversation had turned to a general discussion about sleep, then about dreams, and what they meant, where they came from. Ben and Derek took the position that they were simply the result of the day's information sorting itself out in sleep. But Miranda and Paula argued that dreams often meant something.

"Tell them about the weird nightmares you've been having, Miranda. See what they make of *those*," Ben said, refilling their glasses.

"They're not weird. They're – " Miranda searched for the word – "disturbing. And I never referred to them as nightmares, Ben."

He raised his eyebrows and gave a little laugh. "No?"

"She told me about them," said Paula. "They're worry dreams about the kids. I had them, too, after my kids left home."

Miranda shook her head in doubt. "I don't know. I'm not sure about that. I've thought about it, and I'm really not worried about Clara and Michael. They're both doing fine, and are happy, excited."

Ben leaned in to Derek and Paula. "She's been having them ever since she went to one of those shelters. I told her not to go back, but she has."

"That's not it either, Ben," Miranda said. "That was just a coincidence."

Derek turned to Miranda. "Well, how do you explain them?"

"Whoa," said Ben, leaning back in his chair, and swirling his wine. "You don't want to hear this. Trust me."

"Ben doesn't agree with my interpretation of my own dreams, so he disparages them," Miranda said, shooting Ben a warning look.

"I think people have a sense of what their dreams are trying to tell them," said Paula. "Miranda must know what her dreams mean."

Miranda gave a firm nod.

Paula scrunched up her face. "So what *do* they mean?"

Just then the doorbell rang.

"I'll get it," said Ben, rising from the table. He soon came back with William. "Look who's here," he said pointedly to Miranda. "He didn't want to come in, but I insisted he have a glass of wine with us."

Paula and Derek greeted William, who smiled but hung back. "I didn't mean to interrupt," he said. "I just wanted to ask if any mail had arrived for me."

Miranda shook her head. "No." She gave a quick smile, and then brushed at the tablecloth.

Ben pulled up a chair and was urging William to try some of the food.

William reluctantly sat down, casting his eyes up at Miranda. "Just for a few moments."

Derek reached over and shook his hand. "Evening, William. You can be the tiebreaker."

"Perfect timing," said Paula. "You're just the person we need. We're trying to settle a dispute about – "

"Oh, let's just forget about it," interrupted Miranda. "How about dessert? We have baklava and I made some – "

"No, no," said Ben. "Let's put it to a vote."

Derek leaned over to William and whispered, "Of course, you must side with the men."

Paula grabbed Derek's arm and pulled him back. "No fair. You must be unbiased, William, otherwise it won't count."

Ben came back from the kitchen with a glass and set it in front of William. "Red or white?"

"Red." He watched his glass being filled. "Thank you."

Ben sat back down. "We've been discussing the significance of dreams. I can never remember mine, but Miranda has been having weird dreams lately – sorry," he said, addressing the tablecloth, "not weird – *disturbing* – and I think it's because she was *disturbed* by spending too much time at a halfway house."

"Too much time? I spent a total of ten minutes there."

Paula spoke over Miranda and Ben's dispute. "William, you're the academic. What's your take on dreams – random brain impulses, or messages from the universe?"

Miranda winced at Paula's choice of words. "Let's forget about it." The conversation had degenerated away from its original idea, and the last thing she wanted was to discuss her dreams in front of William. "Who wants coffee?" She tried to catch Ben's eye, but he was purposely avoiding her. She started to clear the table.

William gave a soft laugh. "I'm afraid I don't know much about the subject." He took a sip of wine.

Miranda had taken some dishes to the kitchen, and on returning to the dining room she heard Ben telling them about her recent dreams.

"She's been having dreams that there's a kid trapped somewhere in a wall or pool or somewhere, and he's calling out to her to help him. It's obvious – she's missing the kids and feeling bad about the kids at the halfway house. Her mind mixes it all up, and the result is nightmares. It makes perfect sense." He turned to William. "But Miranda thinks she has to do something about them. What do you think?"

William shifted in his chair, and shook his head, declining an opinion.

"Oh, no you don't," said Paula. "You must take a position. Your vote!"

Everyone awaited William's response, except for Miranda, who continued to clear away the dishes.

William studied the wine in his glass. "There's so much we don't know about the mind. About a lot of things." He raised his head and addressed Miranda. "What are your thoughts?"

Miranda lifted a few more dishes. "Like you say, there's so much we don't know." She smiled at no one in particular, hoping the discussion was over.

But Ben stubbornly persisted. "Isn't the consensus that dreams are our subconscious minds organizing the input from the day?"

"What else could they be?" asked Derek, in support of Ben.

Everyone looked at Miranda and waited for her to refute their argument. Paula made a sweeping gesture for Miranda to take the floor.

Miranda stood with dishes in her hand, determined to counter Ben's generalization. "Well, what if that's only partly true?" she asked. "What if dreams are also a way we communicate – a way of picking up on each other's thoughts, feelings – even actions?" She studied William's expression as she added these last words. Had his eyebrows contracted ever so slightly, or was it her imagination?

"Gee, I hope not," said Derek. "That could be dangerous." He laughed as Paula punched him in the shoulder.

Ben gave a snort of amusement, bringing out Miranda's stubbornness.

"Well, I know it's true. For me. I know that sometimes I have picked up on other people's thoughts."

"Oh, no," said Ben. "Get ready for the cream cheese story."

Miranda felt her cheeks flush in growing anger. "Okay, Ben, it's a silly example, but to me it's proof."

Paula put her elbows on the table and leaned forward. "Tell us. Come on."

Miranda waved away the request. "No. It sounds stupid when – "

"Oh, come on," urged Paula. "We want to hear it. Don't we Derek?"

"Sure we do."

Miranda wavered, then decided to prove her point. "Well, once I was staying at my sister's house. This was years ago. When I woke up in the morning, I went to the kitchen and saw a box of cream cheese on the counter. And I remembered that I had just dreamed that my sister was searching in her refrigerator for cream cheese. I told her, 'You won't believe this, but I just had a dream that you were looking for cream cheese. Except in my dream there were two boxes.' And she said, 'Well, that's really weird because I *was* looking for a second box. I was so sure I had two, for that cheesecake recipe.'"

Derek waited for more. He turned from Miranda to Paula, and back to Miranda.

Paula gave an exasperated groan. "It's obvious. She picked up on her sister's thoughts."

Miranda thought she had made herself perfectly clear. "I mean – what other explanation could there be?"

"There could be plenty," said Ben. "Maybe she told you the night before that she was going to make the cheesecake."

"No, she didn't."

"Maybe you forgot you had the conversation," Ben said.

"You're just determined to prove me wrong. And maybe that wasn't the best example. But there have been other times, especially with the kids." She turned to Paula. "You know, when you go to call the kids, and just then the phone rings and it's them."

"Exactly," said Paul, slapping her hand on the table in emphatic agreement.

"That never happens to me," Derek said, still looking confused. "So what does the cream cheese have to do with the dreams you're having now?"

Miranda was about to explain, but Ben cut in.

"Miranda thinks there's a pervert out there, locking kids up in closets. And she needs to rescue them. They're calling out to her in dreams." He took a sip of wine, and shook his head. "Crazy."

Again, Miranda felt her cheeks heat up. "What if it was one of our kids in danger, Ben? Wouldn't you want some crazy dreaming mother to try and help them?"

"But it's a dream!" he laughed. "You can't respond to it as a fact. What are you going to do – check every swimming pool in town? Every basement and attic?"

Miranda glanced at William and saw that the color had gone from his face.

"Don't be absurd. I'm just saying…" She shook her head, wanting the conversation to be over.

"I don't know, Miranda," said Derek. "I'm afraid I have to agree with Ben. I mean, even if it's true, how do you know it's in this city? Or state? Or country?" He turned to William. "What do you say to that?"

William gave a barely perceptible shrug. "I see Miranda's point. No one wants the burden of guilt. But like Ben says, there's nothing you can do about it. It's just a dream, after all."

Ben slapped William on the back, and gave a triumphant raise of his chin to Miranda.

Just then the phone rang. As if to prove her point, Miranda stood. "That would be Clara," and she left the room to answer the phone.

Derek opened his mouth and looked at the others. "I don't know, Ben. Maybe there is something to what she's saying."

Ben shook his head. "They call each other all the time."

Paula gathered up a couple of plates and followed Miranda into the kitchen. She placed the dishes in the sink as Miranda hung up the phone.

"Well, that was perfect timing." Paula said. "I think you might have Derek convinced. What did Clara have to say?"

"Wrong number. But they don't have to know that."

They started to laugh, just a little at first, but then harder and harder, until they were bent over, wiping tears from their eyes. Paula was slapping the counter, trying to say, "That look on Derek's face – " but couldn't get it out, which made them laugh all the more.

Miranda wiped her eyes and then opened the refrigerator, took out a dish, and uncovered a cheesecake. She began to cut slices and set two plates of the dessert in front of Paula. "Can you bring those?"

When Paula saw the cheesecake, she burst out laughing anew. She and Miranda were still laughing when they went back to the dining room.

Ben and Derek exchanged looks, wondering what they had missed.

Miranda set the plates down in front of Ben and William. "And for dessert we have – "

Derek interrupted her. "Nooo. Don't tell me – cheesecake."

Paula kissed him on the cheek and set a plate in front of him. "You're getting the hang of it."

Ben gazed deep into his wine glass. He was sure Miranda had somehow orchestrated the whole thing – but he couldn't figure out how.

William stood up. "I hope you don't mind, but I have a few hours of work to put in tonight."

"I thought you were on vacation," Paula protested. "Besides, you have to taste Miranda's cheesecake, William. It's divine."

Ben had walked to the wine rack and was searching for a bottle. He stood now with a bottle of port in hand and held it out in front of him as he read the label. "And we have this dessert wine the kids gave us for – was it Christmas?"

"Anniversary," said Miranda. She felt Ben was taking every opportunity to goad her.

William pushed in his chair. "Thank you, but I think I'll turn in. Goodnight."

Ben handed the bottle to Miranda. "I'll show you out, William."

*

Half an hour later, Miranda was cleaning up the kitchen while Ben finished loading the dishwasher and turned it on. Then he noticed that there were still two pieces of cheesecake left and he started in on one.

Miranda had determined to let things blow over, but she felt she had to let off some steam. She spun around and faced Ben, taking him by surprise. "I hate it when you belittle me in front of people." She gave him two seconds to respond, and then began to wash the wine glasses by hand.

"I never belittle you. I was just disagreeing with your argument. That's different. You've become obsessed with these dreams. It's ridiculous."

"Any time I see things differently from you, it's *me* who's the ridiculous one. I'm tired of it." She opened a drawer for a dishtowel, and slammed the drawer much louder than she meant to, causing Ben to look up.

"You know, Sam asked me if I wanted to go to the cabin this weekend for some fishing, and I said no because – "

"I hope you didn't say no on my account. I think it's a great idea. We could use a few days apart."

"I couldn't agree more. I'll tell him I'm coming."

"Good."

"Fine."

"Fine then!"

Ben turned to set the plate in the sink and knocked over a half-filled bottle of wine with his elbow.

Miranda jumped at the sound, and then groaned wearily as the red wine drained onto the counter.

Ben grabbed some paper towels. "I'll get it."

Miranda set the dishtowel down, and watched Ben mop up the mess. Then she went upstairs.

She took a quick bath, and climbed into bed. Disappointed in the way the evening had turned out, she welcomed the heaviness of sleep coming over her. She didn't want to be awake when Ben came in. She just wanted to forget about everything.

Though she tried to empty her mind, she kept seeing the odd expression William had given her when they were talking about dreams. Nor could she forget his guilty look at the pool when he saw her. She felt her mind connecting the dots, an image beginning to emerge that she didn't want to look at.

Again that night, she dreamed that she wandered through the old outbuilding.

She climbed a twisting flight of steps, getting closer to the boy's cries. Near the top, she saw a doll that looked like Clara's. She picked it up and continued along a narrow hallway.

The cries were coming from behind a paneled wall of doors and cupboards, but there were no knobs. She ran her hand along the seams and called out, "Johnny!" She knew the boy was trapped there. Then she saw Ben coming up the stairs.

"Ben," she cried out, "he's here! Behind the wall."

Ben looked at her, then noticed a piece of cheese-cake setting out on a table, and began to eat it.

Miranda woke from her dream and sat up in bed. She looked over at Ben, and knew that she was on her own. She cocked her head and listened. Was that a cry?

She crept out of bed and went to the window that was cracked open; she lifted it higher, and listened. Then she walked to the other window and peered down at the dark garden house. She listened again, but didn't hear anything. After straining to hear any sound, she finally gave up and went back to bed. Sometime in the early morning, she finally fell back asleep.

Chapter 9

~

Miranda briskly swept the driveway, deep in thought about the previous night. The argument with Ben, the tension she felt from William, the dream. And Ben leaving early that morning without saying goodbye. He had never done that before. She stared out at the driveway, wondering if it was all downhill from here.

And yet she was glad Ben was gone, she thought, resuming her sweeping. She needed time alone to figure things out.

"Morning, Miranda!" Paula was crossing over to her with a platter in her hand. "I wanted to return this to Nicole, but no one was home. I haven't seen her or the kids for a while. Have you?"

Miranda glanced over towards Nicole's house, and shook her head.

Paula's expression changed on seeing Miranda close up. "Is everything all right?"

Miranda wondered if she looked as haggard as she felt. "Oh, fine. I just couldn't sleep last night."

"Well, it got to be pretty late. We had a great time. That moussaka was delicious. And it was nice seeing William again. He's such a nice guy."

Miranda focused on the driveway and swept the pine needles and leaves in a pile.

"Sure you're okay? You didn't have another bad dream, did you?"

Miranda brushed it off as of no concern. "Ben left for the peninsula for a few days. Fishing with Sam. Just as well. We were starting to get on each other's nerves."

Paula laughed. "Well, some time apart can be the best thing. Hey, why don't you stop by for dinner? Derek's bowling tonight."

"That'd be nice. Anything I can bring?"

"No, I'll do the cooking for a change." Paula started to leave, but then turned around. "I meant to ask William last night – I thought he said he didn't know anyone in Seattle. Does he have family here?"

"I don't think so. Why?"

"I've seen him outside the daycare once or twice, like he was watching for someone."

"Huh. I don't know. I'll have to ask him," Miranda said, starting to sweep again.

"Seven o'clock?" Paula asked.

Miranda nodded and waved goodbye. She swept more forcefully, not sure if she was trying to suppress an idea or dislodge one. After finishing the driveway and sidewalks, she glanced across the street again at Nicole's house. Now that Paula mentioned it, she hadn't seen Nicole or her kids for quite a while.

She crossed the street and walked up to Nicole's house. The curtains were open, yet everything was quiet. She rang the doorbell and waited. Then she used the knocker. After a few moments, she stepped back and looked for anything unusual. She looked down at her feet, letting her mind follow several possible threads, each unlikely but –

"Hi, Miranda!" called Nicole from the sidewalk. "Is everything okay? You look deep in thought about something."

"Oh, hi!" Miranda said, trying to cover being startled. "Paula just tried to return a dish to you and said she hasn't seen you in a while. I heard that the flu or something was going around at the daycare and I just wanted to make sure the kids weren't sick or anything." She realized she was still holding the broom in her hand.

"The flu?" Nicole asked, tilting her head. "No, the kids are fine. But that's so sweet of you to worry about them. We've been around, just busy with play dates and swimming lessons. We were just down at the park."

Miranda leaned over to the kids. "Did you have fun?"

"Yeah," said Danny. "William pushed me high on the swing, all the way up to the sky."

Nicole laughed. "We run into William now and then at the park. I always tell the kids to leave him alone – he's always busy on his laptop – but he doesn't seem to mind. He's such a nice guy. Has a real way with kids." Nicole unlocked her door. "How about a cup of coffee? I need one after chasing these two all morning."

"Oh, thanks, Nicole. I need to get back and finish up."

"Jack's planning his summer barbeque bash. I'll let you know when the date is. Maybe you could bring William along, if he's still around."

Miranda smiled. "We'll be sure to be there."

"Thanks for stopping by. Say hello to Ben!"

Miranda walked back home more disturbed than before she went to Nicole's. And yet Danny and Ariel were fine; so what was her problem? She began to question her motives. Was she becoming a busybody? Forcing an issue that wasn't even there?

It was better to live on the surface, she thought – on daylight facts, on what she could see and touch, on things that could be known – and not go digging around too much in the mind's darkness.

She sat on the bench outside her front door and looked at the mess from yesterday – how had Derek referred to it? A meltdown? Maybe he was right. Maybe they were all right. She was suffering from empty nest syndrome and wouldn't admit it.

After all, that made the most sense. And the dreams were just a part of it, getting jumbled with old memories: the girl at the shelter stirring up the memory of the girl from grade school; the swimming pool dream mixing with the memory of her childhood friend and her dog, Jasper. All very logical.

It all made sense. And yet.

She bent down and cleaned up the mess, separating the usable pieces of china and throwing away the rest. She stood with the broom in her hand, letting her mind run over the past few weeks. Some things she could make sense of. But everything concerning William was becoming increasingly murky, increasingly troubling. She could not rationalize away her gut feeling.

*

Ben and his old friend, Sam, leaned on the ferry railing, each holding a cup of coffee. Ahead of them lay the deep-green islands with swaths of morning mist still clinging to the trees, and in the distance, partially obscured by clouds, the coastal mountain range. Ben loved being on the Sound, loved the sailboats, the ferries coming and going, the bracing air – both briny and fresh, mixed with the tarry smell of the wharves.

And yet today, the excitement he usually felt when heading to the peninsula was subdued. He had never left Miranda like that after arguing – without making it up. He called her from the ferry terminal and left a message saying he would be home in a couple of days. He would try to call her again when they arrived. Once he got to Sam's, the reception was spotty at best.

Sam was the only person, other than Miranda, that Ben had ever confided in, and he was one of the kindest, gentlest people Ben had ever known. Sam now asked him what had changed his mind about joining him at the cabin.

"Oh, Miranda and I just need some time apart. She hasn't been herself lately. Ever since the kids left."

"How do you mean? Is she sad? Lonely?"

Ben gazed out at the water. "She seems happy enough. I don't know. A little preoccupied, not sleeping well."

"How's the tenant working out? You said she seemed happy to have the cottage rented out for the summer."

"At first I thought she was. Now – I'm not sure. Sometimes I think maybe she confides in him. You know how private she usually is. He really won her over somehow."

Sam looked over at Ben, then back out at the islands. "You're not worried about this guy and Miranda, are you?"

Ben turned to Sam. "You mean – ?" He smiled and shook his head. "No. Not at all. That's not her way. She's fiercely loyal. We both are. That's part of what keeps us so close."

"Well, then, things will work out. Just give it some time."

Ben stared out at the dark, choppy water. "I'm not even sure what we argued about. She's just been kind of temperamental lately."

Sam gave a low chuckle. "When Elizabeth got in a mood – used to be – I just listened. Just nodded, and heard whatever it was she had to say. Then hugged her. It always seemed to work."

Ben looked over at his old friend. "You miss her, don't you?"

"Every day. For the last ten years."

Ben was sorry he had brought up his own marital problems. They were trivial compared to Sam's loss.

They remained silent for a while, each wandering around in their own thoughts as they looked out at the ferries and boats, the swoop of sea birds.

"A few days apart will be good for you both," said Sam, finishing up his coffee. "Fishing. Always good for the soul."

*

Miranda spent the rest of the day working in the upper garden. Pulling weeds, edging the sidewalk and paving stones, feeding the roses. But instead of feeling better, a mix of emotions vied for her attention. Anger that Ben hadn't woken her to say goodbye. Frustration with herself for being so unfocused. And unease from the growing doubts about William. She was beginning to think that maybe he was not what he seemed. Maybe his kindness and interest in her was a facade. He was a complete stranger after all.

She had seen him arrive home half an hour ago. As she weeded, she kept glancing back now and then to see if he was going to leave again. She felt the need to keep track of his whereabouts.

When Ben returned, she would ask him to check with Doug at work, find out more about this guy. You never really knew about people –

"Hi, Miranda."

Miranda gasped and whipped around.

William took a step back.

Miranda jumped to her feet, rattled by his sudden appearance. "I really wish you would make more noise, William." She tried to say it lightly but it came out sounding harsh.

"I – I thought you must have heard me coming." He held up his laptop. "Just going down to the park to work a little."

Miranda watched him walk past her, then she kneeled back down and pulled at a stubborn weed. "William!"

Her tone surprised herself, as well as William, who stopped and turned.

"Yes?" he asked.

"Do you have family here? In Seattle?"

He waited a moment, before answering. "Why do you ask?"

"Just wondering why you've been parking outside the daycare. Paula said she saw you there a few times." She watched him closely to see how he would answer.

"I was waiting for the dry cleaner to open." He looked at her, as if trying to judge if that answer was satisfactory, then he continued on.

She tossed the weed in a pile. Then she stood and watched him walk towards the driveway. "William!" she called out again, more abruptly this time.

He spun around at the accusatory tone in her voice.

Miranda took a few steps towards him, holding the dirty trowel in her gloved hand. "I thought I heard cries coming from the garden house last night." She wasn't sure she had heard anything. But as she watched him, she wondered why he looked so guilty.

He stood still, eyeing her for longer than she expected. Then he shook his head. "I didn't hear anything." He walked away, more quickly than he usually did, she noticed.

She couldn't put a finger on what exactly it was about him, but something was not right. She just knew it. Maybe midlife angst was clouding her judgment about some issues, and maybe she missed the kids more than she thought – but still, something was not right with that guy.

She sat back on the grass, and tossed the trowel to the ground.

*

"Sure you won't join me?" asked Paula, pouring a little amaretto into her coffee.

"Thanks, no. I had too much wine as it is. Just coffee for me."

"How about another slice?" Paula held out the raspberry chocolate cake with fresh whipped cream.

Miranda held up a hand, ready to decline the offer.

"Come on. Raspberries are good for you."

Miranda laughed and agreed to another piece. "I'm going to have to walk ten miles tomorrow."

Paula placed fresh slices on their plates. "I cut and wrapped some cake for you and Ben, and for William," she said, adding fresh coffee to their cups. "I saw William drive off a little while ago. He's such a nice guy, isn't he?" She sat back down at the table.

"I guess so." Miranda took a bite of the cake.

Paula stopped her fork in mid-air. "What? I thought you liked him."

Miranda chewed slowly, as if considering it. "I do. He seems very nice."

"But what?"

"I don't know. Sometimes I wonder if he isn't *too* nice."

"What does that mean?"

Miranda regretted voicing her doubts. "I don't know. I just get the feeling that he's hiding something. He's very secretive."

"Well, that's his prerogative, isn't it?" Paula took a bite of cake. "Maybe he just went through a bad breakup or who knows what. And needs some time alone."

"You're right." Miranda poured milk into her coffee and stirred it. "You know, I don't trust my judgment anymore." She leaned back in her chair. "I've gotten to the point where I'm beginning to doubt my doubts."

"You're just figuring things out. Go easy on yourself. Life is changing and you just need to catch up with it. Give yourself time."

Miranda nodded and smiled at Paula.

"Did you try Googling William?" Paula was already reaching for her phone. "Let's find out more about him. Maybe that would put your mind at rest."

"Oh, no, Paula. That's okay."

"We might find out something interesting about Mr. William Priestly," Paula said, keying in his name.

"Do you think that's his real last name?" asked Miranda.

"Why not? I knew a Rob Priestly once. Why do you ask?"

"I don't know. Maybe it's a way to give a favorable first impression to people," suggested Miranda.

"Or a bad one," countered Paula. "Here we go. William Priestly."

A college webpage quickly came up. She read bits and pieces as she scrolled down the page. "Taught History a couple of years ago, teaches a survey course in World Literature, blah, blah, blah. Here's a link to a syllabus if you're interested. Involved in several youth organizations..." She shrugged. "Nothing too interesting."

"Does it say which organizations? What age group?"

Paula scanned the information. "Looks like there have been several over the years. Has been published in multiple literary journals...writes under aliases. Huh. I wonder why." She looked up at Miranda. "Not much. Just what they want you to know," she said, taking another bite of cake.

The conversation shifted to Paula's walking routine and how she and Derek were planning to hike the coastal trail in Oregon. After another half hour, Miranda stretched, and brought her cup and plate to the counter. "I should be going. Thanks for dinner, Paula."

Paula lifted the extra slices of cake and handed them to Miranda. "Don't forget these."

"Thanks. If Ben calls me tonight, I'll save it for him. If he doesn't, it's all mine."

Paula laughed and walked Miranda to the front door. "Oh! I almost forgot." She went to the kitchen and came back with an envelope. "A letter for William came to our address. Looks like it's from his school. Here you go."

Paula's cell phone rang and she glanced at the number. "It's Derek."

"Tell him hello. I'll see you tomorrow." Miranda waved goodbye as Paula answered the phone and then closed her door.

Miranda cut through Paula's yard, admiring the purple clematis bordering the driveway. She hoped hers would grow as thick with blooms. As she crossed into her yard, she glanced down at the letter – and stopped in her tracks: William J. Priestly. "Jasper," she whispered. "I knew it!"

Her heart began to beat faster and she hurried to her front door. She looked around before unlocking it, stepped inside, and closed the door. She set the plates of cake and the letter on the table thinking that *if* the middle initial stood for Jasper, then he would have heard her paging him at the pool.

She walked to the living room window, and peered down at the garden house. It was still dark. He was out later than usual.

The phone rang causing Miranda to jump. She ran to the kitchen, relieved to hear Ben. But it was a bad connection and his voice kept breaking.

"Ben, what exactly did Doug tell you about –" She raised her voice, trying to make herself clear. "No, I was over at Paula's. Paula's! Yes. What did Doug say about – " but they kept talking over each other, catching only fragments, and then she lost the connection.

She tried to call him back a few times but the calls didn't go through. She hung up the phone in frustration.

Miranda took a quick bath, and then curled up on the living room couch to read. After a while, she realized that she had read the same page at least three times. She set the book down, knowing she would have a hard time sleeping after the chocolate cake and two cups of coffee. She forced herself to read a couple more pages, and shut the book when she heard a car door slam down below.

She turned off the lamp, and went to the living room window. Standing in the darkness, she parted the curtains and saw that William had again parked his car behind the garden house. A light went on inside. She could see him pass the lighted window.

She stood watching for several minutes, wondering if she was making herself crazy with all her suspicions. Yet some stubborn part of her kept asking – what if? What if I am right? Or partly right? What was he doing down there?

The deck would give her a better view, she decided. She silently slid open the door, stepped outside in her nightgown and bare feet, and then walked to the railing where she could see the garden house. The light was still on, and the shade was up on the window facing the house.

She would try to get a little closer. Put her mind at rest. And then go to bed.

Slowly, she walked down the paving stones that sloped to the garden house. At the bottom she stopped, feeling a twinge of guilt at what she was doing – spying. She wavered for a moment. What would Ben say? She groaned and started to return to the deck.

But after three steps she turned around, and crept closer to the garden house, thinking, I don't care what Ben thinks – I need to know. Careful not to make a sound, she tiptoed towards the lighted window, noticing that it was cracked open. Bit by bit, she inched forward until she was able to catch a glimpse inside.

William was at his computer, his back to her. So, apparently he was alone. She watched him for a few moments, trying to make out what was on the screen. She took a step closer and squinted – they looked like photos of women and, she leaned forward, squinting harder – girls? She couldn't be sure.

She jumped when William suddenly scooted his chair back. Miranda held her breath.

He stood and ran his hand through his hair. Then he went to the suitcase, unlocked it, opened it, and lifted something out. His back was to her, but when he slowly turned, Miranda realized, with a loud gasp, that he was holding a doll.

He jerked his head to the window.

Miranda stepped back and covered her mouth. She watched his reflection in the window; he cocked his head as if listening. Then he moved towards the front door.

Miranda dashed back in the direction of the deck, and crouched behind the rhododendrons, making herself as small as possible. With both hands covering her mouth, she sat utterly motionless, cursing the fact that her nightgown was white.

Had he heard her? Would he come outside to investigate?

She heard the front door open, and footsteps on the porch.

"Hello?" William called out. "Is anyone there?"

Remaining absolutely still, afraid to breathe, Miranda waited until she heard him go back inside and close the door. When she saw the shade being pulled down, she fled across the flagstones, up the steps to the deck, and back inside her house.

With trembling hands, she locked the door. She went back to the living room window and peered through the parted curtain. She could see movement behind the lighted shade in the garden house.

She narrowed her eyes, all her suspicions falling into place. "You sneaky, conniving pervert!" she said softly. "I don't know what you're up to. But I'm going to nail you."

Chapter 10

Miranda remained vigilantly awake through most of the night, and didn't fall asleep until almost morning. The darkness of the day caused her to sleep much later than usual, yet when she awoke, she still felt groggy, her thinking all fuzzy.

She looked out her bedroom window and saw William's car parked behind the garden house. She tried to detect whether there was any movement inside, but it seemed still. Above the garden house, the sky hung heavy and gray, threatening rain.

After dressing, she went downstairs to make a cup of coffee, hoping it would help her to think more clearly. While the water boiled, she placed an English muffin in the toaster, and took out the butter and jam. Deep in thought, she jumped when the toaster popped up. She felt as if hands were pulling at her, poking at her, trying to get her attention from all sides. What? she wanted to ask. What is it I'm supposed to do? To know?

She leaned against the counter and ate her breakfast, going over what she had seen last night. Had she overreacted? No. This time, even in the light of morning, her suspicions were strong.

And yet part of her remained mired in doubt.

What had she really seen? There was no proof of anything. But something was not right. No grown man carries around a doll, unless he's up to something. What if he was using it as a lure? And what had he been doing at the pool? Outside the daycare? Why did he look so guilty when she asked him about the cries at night? No. She couldn't let this go. He was a tenant in their house, and that made her responsible.

She stood up straight in resolve. And then slumped back into indecision. What could she do? Watch and observe him? Let him know that she was on to him? He already knew that, she was sure. When Ben returned, she would discuss it with him, and make him understand. She tried his cell phone again, and then dialed Sam's number. No reception.

She filled her time doing laundry, cleaning, tending to the house plants – and checking on the garden house every couple of minutes to see if William was still there. With the impending rain, she knew he wouldn't go walking. She glanced at the clock. He often left in the morning and didn't return until evening – but it was mid-day and his car was still there.

She felt she would go stir crazy if she spent the whole day checking on him. She grabbed her keys and decided to get out. She would run to the store, pick up a few things. Maybe she would call Paula when she got back and invite her and Derek to dinner. This was one day she didn't want to be alone.

While she shopped, she tried to call Ben, but the calls didn't go through. She considered calling Clara or Michael, but she didn't want to worry them. And what would she tell them? No, the best thing was to wait for Ben to return.

Back home, she began to put the groceries away, and reached for the phone to call Paula. A loud rap at the front door startled her. She glanced out the window at the garden house and saw that William had not yet left. Had she locked the door?

Hesitantly, she went to the front door. Then lifting the phone to her ear, she pretended to be in the middle of a conversation, and opened the door.

Paula stood there, smiling. "Hi, Miranda. We decided to head up to Vancouver for a few days. Check out a couple of antique stores and flea markets."

"Oh," said Miranda. She realized she was staring at Paula with a look of alarm. "Sorry – I was just thinking of..." She waved the phone, and smiled. "That's great!"

"Spur of the moment, but those trips are always the best. My sister and her husband are going to meet us there. Just thought I'd let you know."

"Sounds like fun. I'll keep an eye on the house." She walked out to the driveway with Paula and waved over at Derek, who was putting a suitcase in the car.

"We're hoping to make it there before the rain begins. You might want to bring in some of the potted flowers. We're supposed to get quite a storm."

Miranda glanced up at the sky. "Yes. I think I will."

From across the way, Derek tooted the horn.

"I'm coming!" Paula shouted to him. "See you later, Miranda."

"Have a good time!" She walked to the edge of the yard and watched them leave.

Then she went back inside and locked the door. All the vegetables she had bought were set out on the counter; she would go ahead and bake the lasagna she had intended for Paula and Derek. Keep busy. As she cooked, she tried Ben's cell phone again, and looked out the living room window. William's car was still there.

By late afternoon, the sky was growing darker and the wind was picking up. They so rarely had real thunderstorms. But now there was no doubt;

a real storm was building. She looked out at the garden, and worried about the willowy delphiniums and lilies. They would have to be tied, and the tallest flowers staked.

Once the lasagna was out of the oven and cooling, she went outside to take care of her garden. A few drops of rain began to fall as she secured the delicate plants in the upper garden. Then she went back inside and stepped out onto the deck. She placed the potted plants and hanging baskets against the house.

Tentatively, she moved to the railing and peered down at the garden house. Was William not going out? He went out every day. She began to wonder what it meant. Had he known that she was spying on him last night? She rolled up the table umbrella, and brought the cushions from the chairs inside, then locked the door.

After pacing about the kitchen, she decided to work on the mosaic. She took out the bag of china pieces, dumped them on the kitchen table, and began filing some of the edges and setting them aside.

It was early evening when she finally heard a car door slam. She ran to the living room window and saw that William was leaving. Thank God! She let out a deep sigh of relief as he drove off, and realized that she had been holding her breath all day.

Feeling less tense, she made a cup of tea and sat back at the kitchen table. She spread out the mosaic pieces, separating them by color – shades of faded blue, green, and rose – and began to play around with different combinations. But no image or pattern came to her.

Though she tried to concentrate, her mind was all over the place. Maybe the doll was just a gift for someone back East. But it didn't look new. And why was he so furtive about it? What adult gets out a doll late at night?

Something was not right. The feeling of unease that had been with her for weeks – ever since William arrived, she now had to admit – was heightened, urgent. That tapping on the shoulder to pay attention, was now a prod, a push to get out of her head and do something about it. Take some action.

Just then her eyes rested on William's letter. She briefly considered opening it, but decided against it. He wouldn't risk anything incriminating in a letter addressed to the house. Still, she reached for it and examined it closely; it appeared to be of an academic nature. Should she deliver it? No. She pushed it aside, but kept eyeing it now and then. Don't even *think* about going down there, she told herself.

She shifted the mosaic pieces around, drumming her fingers. Then she stood up, and took the key from the kitchen shelf. William would be gone for at least a few hours. And she was just delivering his mail, after all. And the cake from Paula. All very plausible. She would just take a look around, make sure everything was all right, and call it quits. Nothing wrong with that.

She headed down the flagstone steps, sheltering the plate and letter from the raindrops and wind. Decisive action was always better than inaction, she thought. She felt stronger, more in control. It was better to get to the bottom of things, rather than sitting there imagining the worst.

Miranda stepped onto the low porch of the garden house, and even though she knew no one would answer, she knocked loudly.

After a moment, she tried the door and found that it was open. Did William not lock the door? Or did he keep it open in the daytime? She stepped inside, calling out in an overly cheerful voice, "Hello?"

She waited a moment, and then moved to the center of the room.

"Hello? William? Is anybody here?" She stood still and listened. Other than the wind blowing outside, she heard nothing.

She set the plate and letter on the desk near the computer, listened again, and then went to the door and looked outside. She was about to close the door, but then realized that she wanted it open. And though the evening was growing dark, she decided against turning on the overhead light or

the lamp. She didn't want to call attention to herself, and she would only be there a minute.

She went back to the desk and picked up
some folders. Beneath them was a cell phone. Had
William forgotten it? Did he have two? She sifted
through the folders. Notes for different projects, a
drafted syllabus. Nothing out of the ordinary.

In the waste basket next to the desk, she
noticed some crumbled papers. She lifted them out,
spread them open, and tried to smooth them. They
were lists of addresses, some of them circled, others
crossed out. Most were relatively close to the neighborhood, though others were much farther away in
Bellingham and Redmond. She was sure they were
home addresses, not businesses. What did they mean?
Again, she had the feeling that something was not
right. She opened the desk drawers, but except for a
few pens and paper clips, they were empty.

Next to the bed she saw the suitcase. Over-
coming her revulsion, she lifted it and placed it on
the desk. She tried to open it, but it was locked.
She drummed her fingers on the desk, and then
turned in a slow circle, observing the objects in the
garden house. I don't even know what I'm looking
for, she thought.

She walked to the back and glanced into the
bathroom and behind the shower curtain, and then
looked around the kitchen. Then she opened the
door to the back, walked out onto the gravel where

the car had been parked. She bent over and examined the dirt, the clumps of flowers, the threshold, the door itself. Nothing.

Then she went back inside and stood in the center of the main room. The light was fading now and casting the wall of cupboards in a shadowy gray. She shivered as she realized how similar they were to the ones in her dreams. She closed her eyes to better focus on the feeling from the room – and snapped them back open, flooded with a sense of the little boy in her dreams. Her nerves tingled with the sensation of entrapment and fear.

"Hello?" she called out.

Silence.

She walked up to the cupboards and paused before the largest one. Then she slowly opened it. There were the kids' skis and a large basket holding their lacrosse things. Why was she doing this? She knew what was in each of these cupboards. She and Clara had organized them just a couple of months ago. And yet she opened one after another. There was Michael's tent and camping gear. She opened each cupboard, finding it all as she had left it. Nothing had been disturbed.

She was just about to leave when she noticed the ladder-like steps leading up to the loft. She blinked at them a few times, wishing she had brought her cell phone. See it through, she told herself.

She moved to the steep steps, grasped the railing, and began to climb, one step after another, each one squeaking as she placed her foot on it. It had been a while since she had been up there. On reaching the top, she peered over; and breathed a sigh of relief. There was the futon on the floor. A small dresser. Nothing else.

Then she looked at the wall to the left, where a storage area had been built, a low closet that sloped with the roof. She and Clara had forgotten about it. She tried to remember when they had last used it. Should she wait for Ben?

She hesitated a moment, then climbed onto the loft floor, and had to stoop over in the hot, close space. There was a small lamp by the bed that she tried to switch on. She turned the knob again and again, before accepting that the bulb was burned out.

Her heart pounded as she walked over to the cupboard, and she could feel the pulse beating in her neck. A tiny trickle of sweat rolled down her back.

"Hello?" she asked, her voice small and weak.

She made herself move over to the wall, and stooped even more to open the low door. Her hand shook as she placed it around the handle. Holding her breath, she opened the door, and peered into the darkness.

Gradually, the shapes became recognizable: stacked boxes, board games. There was Clara's old dollhouse behind the boxes. She ran her hand over the boxes and examined the dust on her fingertips. Nothing had been moved here for a long time. With a deep release of breath, she closed the door. She climbed back down the steps, her hand sweaty as she held on to the railing.

When she reached the floor, she realized she was still trembling. Her stomach was fluttering in nausea at the vague images she had feared to find. Her hand went to her stomach, pressing it, as if trying to quell the fear. What had she expected really?

Miranda let out a deep breath. She had done what she came for, and could leave now. She just wanted to go home, be back in her house.

Was that a noise? Or the wind?

Her eyes fastened on the low, narrow closet in the back corner. More of an air shaft for pipes and – she didn't really know what. They had never used it for anything.

Again, she was overwhelmed by a sense of fear. But she had come this far. She had to look. And yet she stood rooted to the floor.

Just get it over with, then go home, and wait for Ben, she told herself. Again, the nausea mounted in her stomach.

Step by step, she crossed the room until she stood in front of the closet. She looked for a way to open the door – but the knob or handle was missing. Suddenly she felt she was in her dream, and a rush of prickles crawled over her. She stared at the closet, deciding what to do. She ran her hand along the side of the door, and then pressed over the impression where the knob had been. The door popped open. She pulled it wide.

With her heart banging high in her chest, she bent over and stuck her head inside, craning her neck to see how high the shaft went up. It was dark, but it appeared to be empty. She tapped on the wood inside, to see if any of the boards were loose. She raised her head further up, and on impulse called out, "Johnny." Then again, louder. "Johnny!"

She closed her eyes and listened.

Bang!! The front door slammed shut! She jumped and hit her head as she backed out and straightened.

There was William.

His hair disheveled by the wind and rain, a look of alarm in his eyes, he stood by the door. He seemed to be shaking. Or maybe it was her. His eyes were fixed on her.

"M-Miranda? Wh-what are you d-doing?"

Miranda broke out in a dizzy sweat. She had never heard him stutter before.

William glanced around the room, then back to Miranda. "W-what – why – "

"I brought your mail. You asked for it, remember? And Paula made you some cake. I – I thought I heard a squirrel or something trapped back here."

William moved forward, and looked in confusion at his suitcase on the desk, the papers that had been taken out of the waste basket.

"W-Why – why…," he stuttered, bringing his hand to his forehead and rubbing it.

While his head was in his hand, Miranda skirted the room and made her move to the door.

"Sorry to run, but I think I hear Ben returning." She darted out the door, and ran up the darkened path to her house, casting a wary look behind her.

Reaching the top, she looked behind her, but William had not followed, as she had feared. As she entered the house, the wind caught the door and slammed it loudly behind her. She gave a cry of alarm, and quickly locked it.

She ran to the living room window, and watched the garden house for several minutes, waiting for something to happen. But there was no movement. She wiped at her rain-spattered face, and wrapped her arms around her.

What just happened? she thought, pressing on her heart, as if to still its pounding. Nothing happened. There's no reason for me to be so afraid. Nothing happened.

Perhaps the wind had slammed the garden house door, and it hadn't been slammed in anger. She thought of William's face, his stuttering. He hadn't seemed angry or violent – but he was clearly upset. Did he think she had found something? What had she missed?

Nothing happened, she said again. And yet one thing is now certain: He knows that I know. There could be no more pretense.

She tried to call Ben, but again there was no service. She hung up in frustration. Keeping the phone in her hand, she went back to the living room, and peered down at the garden house. The wind bent the plants and flowers, but there was no sign of movement inside. She closed the curtains.

After a few minutes, she went through the house and made sure all the doors and windows were locked. Against the storm, she told herself. Of all times for Ben to be gone. And Paula. She never felt so alone in her life. Should she call the kids? What would she say? I have no proof, but I think we're housing a –

Miranda shook her head; she was so close to piecing it all together, but she still didn't know exactly what she was looking at. And yet her gut feeling had never been so strong – constricted, bunched up like a fist. She just knew – something. She wrung her hands in anxiety as she paced the living room and kitchen.

She glanced at the clock. It was getting late. Would William leave again? Why had he come back so soon? To catch her? Or had he come back for his cell phone?

She went to the living room window again, and parted the curtains a crack. A light was on in the garden house, but the shade was drawn. She kept her eyes on it, waiting to see what William would do. But after a while, her legs grew tired and she sat on the couch.

The rain began to fall heavily. A thrashing storm, not the usual soft pattering of rain. Wild gusts, branches scraping, a sudden pelting of rain against the windows. She shivered at the sounds.

Again and again, she tried to call Ben, but kept getting the message that the caller was out of range. Realizing the futility of pacing the house and looking out the window, she finally went upstairs to bed.

She decided to keep on her fleece pants and sweatshirt. Why? she asked. Because I'm cold? In case I have to run? Do I keep my shoes on?

From her darkened bedroom, she looked out the window at the garden house. The streaked rain and matted leaves on the window made it difficult to see anything. She thought she could see movement behind the lit shade, but couldn't be sure. It could be shadows caused by the moving tree limbs. Down below in the garden, the bushes and flowers shuddered and churned in the dark wind and rain.

Holding onto her cell phone, she climbed into bed and pulled the blanket around her. Outside the window, the trees swayed and creaked.

She tossed restlessly for what seemed like hours, but when she checked the time she saw that only an hour had passed. Eventually, she drifted into a fretful sleep.

As so often happened, the sounds of the night worked their way into her mindscape, and the creaking of the tree branches found its way into her dream.

The rhythmic squeaking sound was disturbing her sleep, so she left the house to find the source of the sound. It seemed to be coming from the garden. She walked down the path to the garden house, the creaking sound growing louder.

She stepped up to the garden house, and gently pushed open the door – and covered her mouth in horror. There was William's lifeless body hanging from the rafters, the body still swaying and causing the rafter to squeak.

Miranda woke with a start and sat bolt up in a flash of understanding. She put her hands to her mouth as all the pieces finally came together.

"Oh, my God!" She threw off the covers. "Oh my God, oh my God," she cried as she ran down the stairs. She grabbed a jacket from the hall tree and held it over her head before dashing out into the storm.

Nearly blinded by the rain, she ran down the flag stone steps, all her recent dreams converging in her head. How could I not have known?! How could I be so blind? Please let me not be too late!

As she neared the garden house, she saw a pale light through the curtains. She ran up to the porch and put her hand on the doorknob. Her hand shook as she grasped the doorknob, afraid of what she might find. She pushed open the door.

William was packing. Placing his folded clothes into his suitcase. Not at all surprised that Miranda had opened his door in the middle of a stormy night. After a moment, he stopped and turned his face to her.

Their eyes locked in silent understanding, his eyes full of pain and infinite sorrow.

Miranda dropped the dripping jacket to the floor, and slowly walked up to him. With a wounded look in her own eyes, her voice trembled as she softly spoke. "*You're* Johnny."

William turned away from her, still holding the folded clothes.

"Oh, my God, William. I'm so sorry! I didn't mean to intrude. I thought – I thought – I'm so sorry."

Still not facing her, he asked, "How – how did you know?"

"I didn't. I didn't know. I just kept having dreams. Disturbing dreams about a little boy – a little boy who was trapped, and I thought he needed help. And a girl who – "

Miranda stopped. At the mention of a girl, his whole bearing changed. His mouth began to quiver.

"Kristina," he whispered, crumpling onto the couch. "My sister. Kristy." A choking cry escaped him. "I – I don't know what happened to her. I can't find her." He buried his face in his hands, deep, heaving sobs of sorrow pouring through his fingers.

Miranda gently sat next to him, and kept murmuring, "I'm so sorry, William. I'm so sorry."

As William rubbed at his eyes, his cheeks, Miranda noticed, for the first time, the small circular scars on his hands. He began to speak disjointedly, stuttering, struggling to find words.

"I – I couldn't protect her. I tried. But. Sh – she gave herself – so that I – she – "

For a few jumbled moments, a confused rush of words and sobs fought for dominance in William. Then he seemed to give up, and sat utterly still.

He reached for a folded towel and handed it to Miranda. She draped it around her shoulders, realizing she had been shivering. He took another, and roughly wiped his face.

Then he leaned forward, his head in his hands, eyes fixed on the floor.

"Our mother was sick – was dying. She didn't know what was happening to us. He – our stepfather – at first, he just bullied us, beat us. Then one day, at the public pool, it began. He started – he started to – he said it was going to be one of us. Kristy said to use her. And so he did. And anytime I tried to speak out, he made it worse for her."

Miranda felt sick to her stomach as she filled in the blanks, and felt the depth of sadness and pain in William.

After a span of silence, he continued, speaking softly. "When Mom died, they separated us. A great-aunt took me away. Another relative was supposed to come for Kristina. I didn't want to leave Kristy. But they made me get in the car. She waved goodbye to me – and that was the last time I saw her. I later found out that she ran away that day. She was fourteen. I was twelve."

In the silence, Miranda tried to imagine the loss and suffering and fear that must have filled the young brother and sister.

"And you – you never heard from her?" Miranda didn't want to press on his wound, but she wanted desperately to know, to help him, if she could.

William looked up and wiped at his face again. "I did. She sent postcards – for several years. From different cities. They always read: 'I'm fine. Please don't try to find me.' Then one year, they just stopped. But I've never stopped searching for her." His voice quavered, and he pressed the heels of his hands on his eyes. "I don't even know if she's still alive."

He sat quietly for a long while, staring out at the past. Then he took a deep breath, and shook his head. "I spent years wandering the streets of the places the postcards were from – New Orleans,

Atlanta, San Francisco, Portland. At one point, I hired a private investigator. But he couldn't find anything. He said she must have changed her name. Then a few years ago, I began using the internet to search for her."

Only now, back in the present, was he able to look at Miranda. "There are websites for finding missing persons. I've been in correspondence with so many people who thought they might have known Kristina. One or two women I thought might even be her."

Miranda nodded at him in hope, wanting it to be true.

He leaned back on the couch, crushed. "I was *so sure* this time. That's why I came out here. I've been on the trail of someone named Tina, someone with children. The name, the age, certain details. I was so sure. From things said about her, I knew she was living in Seattle. I thought she might even be in this neighborhood. I gave out this address, to let her know that I was here."

Then he slowly shook his head in anguished defeat. "I've sent so many emails, checked so many addresses, hoping – but I always come up empty." His entire body slumped, overcome with weariness, utterly drained. "Maybe it's time I accepted the truth. Either she doesn't want to be found – or she's no longer alive."

He stared out at the floor for a long time, then he took a deep breath and turned to Miranda. "I'll be heading back East."

Miranda watched him, knowing there was nothing she could do or say that would help. "What will you do?"

"Go back. Prepare for classes. Continue with my work. I've spent years working with youth groups – trying to prevent kids like her from ending up on the street."

Miranda put her head in her hands, filled with remorse at her earlier suspicions.

"I'm so tired," William said, leaning his head heavily against the back of the couch. "I'm just so tired."

"Sleep now, William. I'll leave you. But please don't leave yet." She reached out and stroked his head, as she would have done with one of her children. "Sleep now. We'll talk in the morning."

Miranda turned around before leaving and saw that his eyes were closed. She quietly left and closed the door behind her.

Chapter 11

~

Though Miranda had risen early and was waiting for William, it was late morning before he knocked at her door. When she saw him, she noticed a different appearance about him. Less tense, more rested. Yet perhaps a bit sadder, and more resigned.

"Morning, Miranda." He gave a small smile and looked down at his feet.

"How are you, William? Were you able to sleep? How about some breakfast?" She opened the door for him to come in.

He shook his head and remained standing outside, glancing around at the signs of the recent storm. "I did sleep. Deeply. I can't remember the last time I slept so late."

"Are you sure you don't want some coffee?"

"No. Thanks. I just wanted to say – I'm sorry you got caught up in my problems. I didn't mean for that to happen."

"It was all my doing, William. Ben always accuses me of going too far with my ideas."

He rubbed his brow. "But – how did you know? Why did you call out my name? No one has called me Johnny for years."

"I thought I heard it, one night. Someone calling out that name. I'd been having dreams about a little boy. So that's how I began thinking of him – as Johnny. I'm afraid I was way off track, guessing all sorts of things – and then, suddenly, everything just clicked last night. And I knew that *you* were the little boy."

William listened, his brow smoothing as she explained. "I thought my past was written all over me. I've always felt like I was branded. I thought you picked up on it from the beginning."

"No, William, not at all. It was just me, missing the kids, worrying about them, getting tangled up in my doubts." She paused before adding, "Though, I was sure I heard cries coming from the garden house – on two or three different nights."

William rubbed his shoe on the flagstone. "I – I used to wake myself up screaming, crying. I thought it had stopped. But lately, it's been happening again. I keep dreaming that I finally find Kristy – but that she runs away from me."

Miranda lowered her head. How could she have so misjudged him? That tentative, secretive air about him was just his way of protecting his wound, the way he carried the burden of guilt and sorrow that had never left him.

William took a piece of paper from his pocket, marked with circled addresses. "I'll finish what I started. I have a few more addresses to check out. Two in north Seattle, one up in Edmonds. One last try, before I head back East."

Miranda saw the struggle. Part of him was trying to remain hopeful, but another part had already accepted defeat.

He looked down at the piece of paper. "I don't have much hope. The dates don't add up." He put the list back in his pocket and forced a smile. "I'll be back by evening. Then I think I'll head out. It's time I got on with my life."

"Won't you wait a little longer? Ben will be back later today."

William nodded. "I won't leave without saying goodbye to him."

He hesitated a moment, then opened his laptop bag. "I'm wondering if you'll take care of something for me." He took out the battered doll, and handed it to Miranda. "It's time she had a real home."

Tears shot to Miranda's eyes as she reached for the doll. "Of course, I will."

"Thank you, Miranda." William quickly turned and got in his car.

She watched him leave, thinking that she would try to talk him into staying for a few more days. Maybe Ben could convince him. She didn't want him to leave feeling so sad. Though he seemed determined to move on with his life, she knew that he would never give up searching for his sister, or finding out what happened to her. It would be a life of no rest, no peace.

Miranda gently placed the doll on the window shelves, between the pink kalanchoe and a small jar of forget-me-nots. "I'll take good care of you," she said.

She opened the door to the deck and moved the potted plants back out into the sun, and hung up the flowering baskets. Then she swept away the leaves that the storm had brought down.

Once the deck was taken care of, she slipped on her shoes, and went out to inspect the garden, picking up branches and clumps of leaves. For the most part, the flowers had weathered the storm well; they always appeared so delicate, and yet were astonishingly resilient.

Throughout her garden, sunlight sparkled on the wet leaves and stones, and glistened on the black iron fencing. All around the rose bushes, delphiniums, and tall phlox lay pools of petals in pink, blue, white. As she gazed out on the garden, and back at the house, she saw what William had described to her that day in the garden: Home – and she felt overwhelmed by her deep love for it, for all the memories that were a part of it.

Thinking of William and his sister, she walked back to the spot where she and William had talked that day. As she looked at the bench, she had the idea that it would be perfect for the little garden at the shelter. She would paint it first; or perhaps paint it with Zoe at the shelter.

As she meandered through the garden, she saw other items she could take to the shelter: a birdbath that would give some height and interest to the garden, two or three clay sculptures that could be tucked under some of the plants, maybe a birdhouse or two. Just a few small items would transform the little garden.

Her mind leapt in multiple directions, imagining Zoe and the other teens painting the bench, one of the other girls filling the birdbath. Or maybe she would teach them how to make some mosaic stepping stones, or one of the painted screens that they could use for the entryway at the shelter. Perhaps their lives were not unlike that of Kristina's.

She just wished she could do more for William. But for now, she decided, walking back to the house, she would bake cookies for him – a small gesture of home that he could take with him.

Miranda returned to the house, and began mixing the batter, thinking of Ben and of how much she missed him. As she was spooning the dough onto a cookie sheet, the phone rang. She reached for it and saw that it was him.

"Ben! I've missed you so much! Where are you? When will you be home?"

"Maybe I should leave more often," laughed Ben. "We're heading to the ferry now. I'll be home by evening."

"I love you, Ben. I have so much to tell you. I miss you."

"I miss you, too," he said, his voice filled with warmth.

Miranda kissed the phone before she hung it up. She put the first batch of cookies into the oven, counting the hours until Ben would be home. She couldn't wait to hold him tightly, and to feel the world settle back into place.

She had just taken out the last batch of cookies and set them on the counter to cool, when the doorbell rang. She looked up at the clock; it was too early for Paula and Derek to be back.

When she opened the front door, she was surprised to see a man and a woman standing there, with two little girls at their side.

Miranda looked at the woman more closely, and her whole body tingled. The woman was pretty, but had a sad, worn look about her; her resemblance to William was unmistakable.

The woman spoke in a soft, low voice. "I'm sorry to bother you. I'm not sure if I have the right address." Her voice began to tremble, and the man beside her put his arm around her protectively, as if giving her courage.

"I'm Kristina Bergstrom. This is my husband, Pete. And our daughters." She smiled down at the little girls. "I'm looking for someone named Johnny Priestly."

"Oh, my God," said Miranda, holding on to the door. "Please, come in. Come in. William will be back soon."

Kristina hesitated, unsure of whether to follow. "I'm not sure I have the right person, but Pete said we should just go and find out."

"Please, come inside," Miranda said again, trying to remain steady, but she was shaking with sheer joy.

Kristina lifted her face to the barrel-chested man next to her.

"It's all right, Honey," he said. "Let's just go in." He smiled down at Miranda. "Thank you, ma'am."

Miranda bent over to the little girls. "I just baked some cookies. Do you like chocolate chip?" She led them all into the kitchen and was just about to offer coffee when she heard a cry.

Kristina's hands covered her mouth – she was staring at the doll on the shelf. She swayed dizzily and held onto her husband.

"Oh, my God, Pete. It *is* Johnny." She walked slowly to the shelves. Her hand trembled as she reached up, and she wavered before taking the doll in her hands. Then she broke down.

Pete put his arms around her. He looked at Miranda and down at the girls, and then said quietly, "Sit down, Honey. I'll take the kids outside."

"The door to the deck is open," Miranda said, pointing to the living room. Here," she said, offering him a plate of cookies. "Take these. And there's a swing down in the garden."

The girls looked up at their mom with big worried eyes.

"Come on, girls," Pete said. "Mommy needs to be alone for a minute."

Kristina turned to her daughters and wiped her tears away. "It's okay. Go with Daddy. I'll be out in a little bit."

Miranda poured a glass of water and set it in front of the woman, and then sat in the chair next to her.

"I don't understand," Kristina said. "Do you know Johnny? Is – does he live here?" She looked around, as if expecting him.

"He's staying here as a guest. He came about a month ago." Miranda clasped and unclasped her hands, unsure of how much she should say. "He – he's told me a few things. He told me he came to Seattle to look for his sister."

Kristina stared at the table, shaking her head. "Are you sure he's coming back? When will he return?" Her eyes wandered around the table, and she kept bringing her hand to her mouth.

"I think he should be back in an hour or two." She looked at the clock. "Maybe sooner."

A shadow of worry filled Kristina's eyes, and she glanced up again and again at the clock. Her voice trembled as she reached for a tissue from her purse. "It's been so long. He may not – I don't know if – " She kept wiping at her eyes, and putting her fingers to her forehead, in disbelief.

"Let me make some coffee," Miranda said. "Or would you prefer tea? Or – something stronger?"

Kristina now rested her eyes on Miranda, as if only now really seeing her. She took a deep breath and smiled. "You don't even know me. And you're being so kind. I would love some coffee. Thank you."

While Miranda made the coffee, she saw that Kristina kept dabbing at her eyes, while gazing at the doll.

"I can't believe he kept it all these years." She looked up at Miranda. "Did he tell you – "

Miranda turned and nodded sympathetically. "It came out after – it's a long story. But, yes, he told me some of what happened."

Kristina's shoulders loosened, as if relieved that she didn't have to explain anything.

They could hear the laughter of the girls and Pete from out on the deck. Kristina took a deep breath and her tension seemed to lessen. Little by little, over their coffee, Kristina told Miranda pieces of her past.

"I wanted to find Johnny. I knew he had looked for me when…" She let her words drift off, and gazed down at her hands, into the past. "There was a time I didn't want him to find me. I didn't want him to know what…" She struggled with her words, starting and stopping many times. "It was Pete who started the search this time."

"This time?" asked Miranda.

"I tried to locate him many years ago. But I couldn't find out anything. His caretaker, an elderly relative, had died, and he got moved around. But no one seemed to know where he was. I – I didn't know who to turn to. Out of desperation, I contacted – our stepfather." Tears shot to her eyes, and she looked up at Miranda in fresh outrage. "He told me that Johnny had died. And he told it in such cruel detail that I believed him." She looked down, and after several moments she spoke almost in a whisper. "I shut down after that. For a long time."

It took her several moments before she could continue. Then she sat up taller, and took a deep breath, as if shifting from wounded girl to the woman she was now. "It wasn't until I met Pete that I – that I got better, that I began to believe in some kind of a future.

"Our – stepfather – died recently. Until then, I was always afraid. I was afraid he would find my girls. He was a – a sick man." Her face filled with revulsion at the memory of him.

"When Pete first tried to find out what happened to Johnny, it became clear that someone was looking for me, online. I thought it was him – my stepfather. So I avoided those sites, afraid he would be able to track me down."

As if still surprised at the news, she looked up. "Then one day, Pete told me that he had died. He was furious that he didn't get a chance to hurt the bastard before he died. I read the obituary in disbelief. I thought he would always be there – a dark shadow always right behind me. I was afraid it was a trick, and I waited, making sure he was really dead.

"Then slowly, Pete began responding to some postings on different sites. And that's how we found out that Johnny was *alive*, and that he was *here*. I was stunned. I still can't believe it's true."

The sounds of laughter pulled her gaze out to the deck. "Pete's been so supportive. All along." She swallowed, and Miranda followed her eyes to where Pete was sitting with the girls on the deck, making them laugh with some story, then saying, "Let's find that swing."

Kristina's eyes filled with love as she beheld her family. "I never thought I would have so much. Be so happy. And now, to know that Johnny is still alive, and has been searching for me." She looked down at the doll again, as if to confirm that it was all true.

They heard a car pull up outside, and a car door open.

Kristina stood up, clutching the doll. "Oh, God." She placed one hand on her stomach and steadied herself against the table.

Miranda gave her a reassuring smile, and then went to open the front door.

William got out of the car, and walked towards the house. He forced a smile, and shook his head. "Another false lead."

The laughter of the girls and Pete came from the garden, and William suddenly noticed the other parked car. "I'm sorry. I didn't know you had company. I just wanted to let you know that I'll be leaving in the morning – "

Miranda put a hand on his arm. "William – there's someone here for you."

He stared at her, trying to read her expression.

Miranda walked inside, and into the kitchen.

William remained rooted, then tentatively followed her in. When he reached the kitchen, he stopped. Before him stood his sister, clutching her old doll.

He stared, not quite believing. "Kristy?"

"Hello, Johnny," she said timidly.

He rushed to embrace her, as they both broke down.

Miranda left them together, and joined Pete and the girls out in the garden.

Chapter 12

~

In the garden house, Miranda stood in front of the latest of her floral wooden screens. Ben had widened the window over the summer, and the increase in light had inspired her to finally complete the screen she had begun years ago. And the completion of that project had triggered a burst of creative energy that had not diminished.

She had spent the afternoon working on the screen. Now, with a paintbrush in her hand, she studied the composition before her. She added a few dabs of green, a final highlight of gold, and then decided that it was finished. A coat of varnish, and this one would be ready for Paula's shop. She almost hated to part with it, she was so pleased with the way it had turned out. But she wanted to send it out into the world, a little part of herself, of her vision, that might bring pleasure to someone else.

Besides, she had several ideas for others that she wanted to get started on. Paula had sold three screens so far and was waiting for more. Miranda had also finished the mosaic mirror, adding bits of blue and green sea glass, and had made a gift of it to Paula as a thank you for all the encouragement she had given. It now hung in her new store, like a burst of blossoms forming the heart of the shop.

Paula had surprised Miranda with the suggestion that she teach classes. Several customers had expressed an interest in learning how to make the screens and mosaics, and the small floral paintings that were so popular.

It was a possibility Miranda had never considered, but one that filled her with excitement. She imagined holding a class in the garden house – a dynamic day of instruction that would include lunch, and finish up with tea in the garden. Maybe she could team up with other artists – maybe she would seek out the artist woman with the swimming pool. Maybe Zoe could be a part of it somehow. Life was opening up to her, in a thousand possibilities.

Miranda cleaned her brushes and finished up for the day. She gave a final satisfied look at the screen, and closed the garden house door.

A cool, misty rain had pervaded most of the day, but now, as she made her way up the flagstone steps to the house, she saw that it had dissipated. The sun shone on the garden, thick with late summer flowers and early autumn blooms.

Inside the kitchen, Miranda turned on the tea kettle and reached for a cup. The summer's cloud of confusion and doubt had vanished and she could think clearly once again.

Everything was as it should be. Michael and Clara were coming home for a long weekend. William had gone back East after spending every day of the summer with Kristina and her family, and he had decided to relocate to Seattle after the fall semester.

Ever mysterious, William had surprised Miranda one last time before leaving. She and Ben had planned a farewell cook-out for him, and invited Kristina and her family, Paula and Derek, and Nicole and her family; and William had asked if he could bring someone. In answer to her questioning eyes, he had laughed and said simply, "Edmonds. I showed up at the wrong address that day, and I happened to meet an incredible woman."

Miranda made herself a cup of tea and took it into the living room. She turned on the lamp, and curled up in the window seat overlooking the garden. Outside lay a world intensified by the earlier rain – the greens deeper, the soil darker, the flowers brighter.

She took a sip of tea and let her gaze fall over the living room, deriving a deep pleasure from her home. On the mantel stood her Moroccan enameled pottery. A soft glow from the fringed lamp fell on the velvet brocade of the overstuffed chairs. A few vases of russet and purple chrysanthemums sat on the coffee table and among the bookshelves. This feeling of well-being, of being surrounded by love and beauty and family is what mattered most to her. And letting her life intersect with others, like William and Kristina. Like Zoe.

A smile crossed her lips as she thought of William. She still found it hard to believe that she had ever doubted him. It was impossible now to think of him as anything other than the kind, gentle soul she knew him to be.

She sipped at her tea, wondering how she could have been so wrong about so much. Wrong about his character and what he was up to. Wrong about any significance in the name Jasper, other than it being a name associated with a dog and a pool. All the disparate threads of missing the kids, turning fifty, and going to the shelter, had become tangled up with childhood memories, and dream images, and tension with Ben – resulting in a cloudy vision.

And yet, as William had told her, she had been right about much. He said it was as if she had stepped back in time, and helped that child who was trapped and afraid and in need of protection. And that now, as a man, he was finally becoming whole, happy, healed – and eager to embrace her belief that it was never too late to create a place called home.

It *was* never too late.

Miranda set her teacup down with the sudden realization that she hadn't been true to her own convictions. And the thing she had been most wrong about was the insidious, slow-creeping belief that the best years were behind her.

She sat up straight. That's not the way it was going to be. Time had not buried her old self. It was still there, more alive than ever. The summer had served to galvanize her desires and focus her vision.

She would get back in touch with that earlier, excited, hopeful part of herself – the one that painted medieval landscapes, and threw clay, and dressed in Bohemian skirts. She would merge that old self with the way she was now – with her gardening, and experimental cooking, and magical nights with Ben.

Miranda jumped up and decided to make it happen. Now. Today. And every day.

In one of those moments of euphoria that sometimes overtook her, she flashed on a vision of how this night of today would be.

Barefoot, she walked outside into the garden where the late afternoon sunlight cast everything in a soft golden glow. She began taking cuttings – bunches of roses and dahlias and hydrangeas, tall stems of phlox and foxglove, smaller chrysanthemums and asters. Then she cut branches from the laurel and curly willow, and gathered trails of ivy.

Filling her arms and basket, Miranda carried the flowers and greenery into the house, and spread them out on the kitchen table. Then she began arranging the flowers in vases and jars, and floating them in glasses and bowls. She set the containers all around the house: slender bud flutes and cut crystal vases on the shelves and counters, larger earthenware jars with tall branches and flowers on the floor. Small bouquets lined the stairs, fuller arrangements surrounded the entry. Throughout the rooms, the beauty of the garden bloomed.

*

When Ben came home from work that night, he noticed red and pink rose petals strewn along the sidewalk leading to the house. When he opened the front door, he was greeted with strains of exotic music and the aroma of freshly chopped parsley and garlic and lemon and spices. From the entryway, he saw that the dining room table was beautifully set with flickering candles and flowers and a spread of dishes.

He set his briefcase down and walked towards the kitchen. More candles and vases of flowers lined the hallway, filled the counters, and reflected against the mirrors.

"Miranda?" he called out, walking into the kitchen.

Miranda wore one of her beloved old skirts, its sequins glittering in the candlelight as she moved about. Her hair was loosely swept up, with a pink rose tucked behind her ear. Her bare arms showed toned and tanned from the summer, as she poured out two glasses of champagne.

"Hello, my husband!" she said, giving him a full kiss on the mouth and handing him a glass.

Ben laughed and looked all around him. "What's all this? On a weeknight?"

Miranda briefly took in the table, the candles, and the profusion of flowers, and considered what to call it. "It's a celebration!"

"What are we celebrating?"

"Everything!" She raised her glass. "To life. To the kids coming home this weekend. To still being madly in love with you. To not knowing what's up ahead. To – "

"Okay, I get the idea." He wrapped his arms around her. "You make me happy, Miranda."

"Do I?"

"Yes," he said, kissing her. "You always have."

Miranda smiled with excitement. All her old dreams were still fully alive, stronger now for being entwined with new dreams. She could almost feel the fresh shoots and blooms beginning to emerge.

Made in the USA
Middletown, DE
25 June 2018